This book is dedicated
to Nancy and Tom.
The best parents a girl
could have wished for.

x

E. L.

B & B

First published in the UK in 2018 by Nosy Crow Ltd
The Crow's Nest, 14 Baden Place, Crosby Row
London, SE1 1YW, UK

Nosy Crow and associated logos are trademarks and/or registered
trademarks of Nosy Crow Ltd

A CIP catalogue record for this book will be available from the British Library.

Printed and bound in Great Britain by Clays Ltd, Elcograf S.p.A.

Papers used by Nosy Crow are made from wood grown in
sustainable forests.

ISBN: 978 1 7880 0351 3

www.nosycrow.com

TWINKLE TOADSPIT, the Shakespearean actress and witch of MEGA POWER and UNKNOWN POTENTIAL, must comply and conform if she is EVER to perform her very best Bottom.

Summary:

What I ac-chew-ally now know about me:

Fact One: I am currently a pupil at, and future owner of, Toadspit Towers, School of Witchcraft.

Fact Two: I am the wearer of the Rainbow Hat of Awesomeness. The bearer of the Witchwood Thumb. The possessor of the Witchwood Tree Charm that is currently dangling from my Toadspit bracelet.

Fact Three: I have made a Deal of Doom.

Fact Four: I am attempting to be a Pupil of Perfection.

Here is the current update on my current life of tragedy: Being a Toadspit witch is boring and I am a failure as an actress.

I am acting patience. Jess and Shalini are with me but they are *not* acting patience. We are standing in the first-year bathroom, lighting up the gloom with our hat-lights.

There is no sign of Dominique or Arwen, the Best and Brightest and Most Annoying witches of Toadspit Towers, School of Conformity and Strictness. This is a good thing.

I am standing back, pondering on my life of disaster and the Deal of Doom. Shalini is watching Jess. Jess is peering into a toilet. Not the ac-chew-al toilet bowl. That would be foolish. A mistake with consequences. She's peering into a toilet cubicle because some of the toilets have developed a habit of exploding and it's our task to stop that happening. They don't exactly explode like a bomb going off. They gush. Like volcanoes of icy water. Upside down waterfalls of ferocity. At inconvenient times.

Ms Sage suspects that my great-great-great grandma Marietta Toadspit's cat-creature of catastrophe, Jacobus, hexed the plumbing before we trapped him. I suspect Ms Thorn has ordered us to remove the hexes as a punishment for letting the cat out in the first place.

This is the seventh cubicle we've checked, pre-breakfast, for magical mayhem and this is why being a witch is boring. I am an actress not a plumber.

Jess stops inspecting and stands up very straight.

"Step one," she says. "Someone must trigger the spell by sitting on the toilet." She sounds just like Ms Thorn. The deputy headmistress speaks as she looks, slow and emotionless. She points at me. "You must sit."

"I wish you would stop pretending to be Ms Thorn," I say. "It's creepy."

She shakes her head. "I shall not do as you ask until you have conformed and complied with my instructions, followed all my rules and been the most obedient witch in the school."

I do not answer. I peer past her. I cross my eyes and stare at the toilet. "This one looks OK. Let's move on."

She pulls me back by my shirt. "You're only saying that because it's your turn to check," she says in her own voice. She waves her witchwood spoon at me as if she's about to poke me with it. She does. "And you know there is only one way to check for hexes. Sit."

I look to Shalini for support.

She's no help. "Sit," she says. "You know what Ms Sage said. The toilet hex is spreading and if we fail to remove all the hexes today it will spread again tomorrow and we'll have to start all over again."

Oh pimples. I have no time to fix TOILETS! I have to fix my LIFE! I have to ponder on some *Very Important Thoughts*. Worrying thoughts. There are potential disasters to contemplate! My ac-chew-al acting career is in the DIREST DANGER! AGAIN!

I have almost completed the tour of *A Midsummer Night's Dream* with Ms Dench, Mr Marlow and my old drama group from St Bluebottle's School of Creativity and Fun. I have successfully performed seven perfect performances of my Bottom in school halls across the land and it was AMAZING! My donkey's head is now as comfy as my Hat of Awesomeness.

This afternoon we have a dress rehearsal. Tonight, we have our last ever performance only it won't be performed in a school. It will be performed in a real theatre with real, proper theatre seats and a real, proper theatre stage with lighting and curtains and props.

This all sounds great BUT at our very last school performance, performed at The Pleasant Primary Academy a whole week ago … DISASTER struck! Ms Sage did not accompany me to the school. She was not there to clap her enthusiastic sea lion clapping.

Someone else came instead.

Ms Thorn, with her normal deputy headmistress's face of emotional blankness, accompanied me to the school. She sat in the audience. The play began. I heard my cue. I walked on. Ready to perform. I glanced at her and her look had changed! From emotional blankness to a look from *The Book of Disapproval and Criticism* and I immediately FORGOT MY LINES! I FROZE! In front of an ac-chew-al AUDIENCE! This has never ever happened to me before and I keep reliving the moment of horror and I am TOTALLY TRAUMATISED! I have questions.

Question 1: Did Ms Thorn hex me? So that I would forget the lines and give up my acting career?

Question 2: Has becoming a witch altered my brain? Have I added so much witchy information into the zen space in the middle of my magical mind that my ordinary mind is now incapable of remembering lines?

Question 3: Will I freeze, lose the plot, dry up, or get the giggles of nervousness in this afternoon's dress rehearsal?

Question 4: Why did I agree to the Deal of Doom? Why didn't I say: I agree that a Toadspit teacher shall accompany me to each performance – any teacher except Ms Thorn?

Shalini interrupts my *Very Important Thoughts*.

"Stop pondering on your *Very Important Thoughts*, Twink," she says, even though she knows how important they are because I have previously told her. Every day for the last seven days.

Jess has crossed her arms and she's tapping her foot with impatience. "It's nearly time for breakfast and we've only done six loos. SIT."

I give in because they won't give in. I plonk myself on the seat. If there is a hex there's usually a warning gurgle followed by a whoosh of swirling water swooshing up the pipe. I wait for it. They wait for it. We all wait for it. There is no gurgle but suddenly the seat vibrates and *WHOOSH!* I scream.

"Aargh!"

I'm forced off the toilet by an Icelandic geyser of LIQUID ICE!

I fall sideways. Jess catches me. The gush hits the ceiling and splashes back down, soaking us. She screams too.

"Aargh!"

Shalini holds her witchwood spoon over our heads and shouts, "Witchwood, witchwood, do the deed. Change to be what I now need." Her spoon changes into a giant umbrella that covers the three of us. It's green to match her drenched and drippy witch hat. She's laughing.

"It's not funny," I say. I stagger out of the cubicle. I blink the water out of my eyes and lift the brim. I am SOPPING! My Rainbow Hat of Awesomeness is now a soggy Rainbow Hat of Awesomeness and my hair has stretched to twice its normal length with the weight of the water. My shirt and skirt are completely soaked and my tights have gone wrinkly at the knees. This does not improve my mood.

Jess splashes us as she shakes her head like a wet dog, a wet dog with brown hair and a thick fringe. Her hat falls off and lands in the flood pouring out of the door. It floats like a pile of mushy green tea leaves.

"You laughed when I was gushed," she says.

"And me," says Shalini.

"That was different," I say. I grab Jess's hat, wring it out and plonk it back on her head. "That was you. This was me."

The flood is flooding further. It's soaking into my boots.

"Time for *Team Toilet* to go into action," says Jess. She pretends to be Ms Thorn again. "Step two: Once the hex has been triggered Twinkle must be the one to find and remove it. She requires practice at *seeing beyond* to develop proficiency."

"I have practised!" I say. Ms Thorn has had me

practising this particular activity of *seeing beyond* – "eyes crossed and look through the layers" – so much that I worry that my eyes will stay that way for ever. Maybe this is why I forgot my lines! My brain has become crossed inside!

My soggy friends are waiting. As previously mentioned, they are not acting patience. I give in, again, and cross my eyes. My vision shifts. I see a layer of atoms and the space between. I see the layers behind. Layers of colour and shape. I pull and push and slide the layers until the picture comes into focus like switching from two dimensions to three. I see the hex. It's a bright-blue splodge on the side of the toilet bowl, like a raindrop. I imagine what I want to happen. I imagine the corner coming loose. I imagine the hex peeling away like sticky chewing gum. I imagine it blowing up, like a big blue bubble-gum bubble. It bursts and pops into nothing. The gushing stops. I'm getting faster.

Maybe speed will impress Ms Thorn? Maybe my success will remove the look from *The Book of*

Disapproval and Criticism and replace it with a look from *The Book of Approval and Admiration?*

I hear Ms Thorn say, "Step three," and I blink my eyes uncrossed, thinking the teacher has arrived, but it's Jess again. She's looking down as if she's talking to someone.

"Jessica Moss shall practise her drawing skills to drain the excess water. She will use the reality rune and only that rune. Failure to conform and comply will result in complications and possible catastrophe."

Then she looks up as if she's talking to someone. "I shall comply with your instructions, Ms Thorn," she says in her own voice. There is a possibility she has caught "acting" from me.

She points her witchwood spoon at the floor. We are now up to our ankles in water. She sketches a plughole on the floor, through the water. It glows, as if she's drawn it with a green-neon-light pencil.

"By the power of the witchwood, by the power of the spoon, make this drawing real, with the writing of this rune," she says.

She draws the reality rune. It looks like half a pointy fir tree. The green glow changes to purple then grey and the image changes to a real plughole. I can see down into it, like looking down the drain in a sink, but bigger. The water gurgles and swirls around and around and into the pipe. The pipe shrinks and the drain disappears.

Jess's drawings never last long. Just long enough to do the job. Unlike Greats-Grandma Ursula Toadspit's scary spider drawings. Her Toadspit Terrors are still stalking the school after three hundred years. She must have used permanent ink. I don't think they'll ever disappear. Not that I've seen them since the night they tried to eat me. Maybe they're hiding in the West Wing, waiting to pounce.

Jess acts Ms Thorn again.

"Step four: Shalini Chandra shall keep a record of which toilets were hexed and which hexes were successfully removed. Shalini must make a precise and detailed report that does not allow for any mistakes that could result in magical mayhem or—"

"Enough!" says Shalini. "I am complying." She's grinning. We both are. I am beginning to wonder if Jess has the Power of Positivity in the way the headmistress, Ms Sage, has the Power of Persuasion.

Shalini turns her spoon into a pencil, straightens her skirt and touches her Pocket of Usefulness. "Fetch map," she says. A map pokes out of her pocket. She opens it out and ticks one of the toilets adding a note about the force of the gush – Force 10. She puts the map back. "Seven down, twenty-one to go," she says.

Twenty-one! I sigh. Is this what my life will become if I fail at the rehearsal later? Shall I have to have a career as a magical plumber? *Twinkle Toadspit: Toilets drained and toilets trained. Text TT if your loo's been hexed.*

I sigh again.

Jess shakes her head at me. "Oh, for goodness' sake, Twink," she says. "Stop the sighing! You've been sighing all week!" She aims her spoon at me and mutters something.

"Of course I have," I say. "I'm having to waste time on toilets while my BOTTOM is DOOMED and Ms Thorn—"

A blast of hot air shoots out of her spoon. I cannot speak. My mouth is full of air. It's like being in a wind tunnel. I hold on to my hat.

"Maybe forgetting your lines was nothing to do with Ms Thorn," says Shalini. "Maybe it was just stage fright. The sort everybody gets." She's standing with her arms out, letting the warm wind dry her clothes. The skin on her face is wobbling.

"Or," says Jess. "Maybe it was the stress of being Ms Thorn's Pupil of Perfection. You've been a mega obedient pupil with your 'Yes, Ms Thorn's and your 'No, Ms Thorn's and your 'Three Bags Full, Ms Thorn's for almost three whole weeks. Maybe it has affected your brain." She peers at my forehead. She aims the dryer at my feet.

"But, Jess, what if Ms Thorn has hexed—"

Jess inspects my face. "I believe too much obedience has unnerved you."

"But she might have cast a—"

"I believe you allowed Ms Thorn to fluster you."

"I know but she'll be in the audience this aft—"

"I believe you should ignore her."

Shalini joins in with the annoying interrupting. "What if someone boos?" she says. "You'd definitely have to ignore that."

What?! Why would someone boo me? Why would she make me worry about that! They are annoying me with their unhelpful suggestions so I talk fast. "But how can I ignore her look from *The Book of Disapproval and Criticism*? What if there's also a look of TOTAL AND ABSOLUTE BOREDOM? There'll definitely be an absence of SMILE and this is a COMEDY! People are *supposed* to smile."

"I'm not sure Ms Thorn *can* smile," says Shalini.

I am Living In The Land of Despair. "And if I fluff my lines Mr Marlow will DEFINITELY give MY BOTTOM to Deirdre Kempe for the *very special* evening performance and I will have to play her part. The part of *THE WALL*! Because *THE WALL* DOES NOT SPEAK! I cannot forget my lines if I have NO LINES!"

"Then there is only one solution," says Jess. She dries her hair with one blast from her spoon.

I wait.

"You   must   make   Ms   Thorn   smile   before

the rehearsal. Get her in a good mood for the performance."

I gasp. That's it!

"Jess, you are a genius!" I am inspired! "I have a plan. I shall train Ms Thorn to smile!"

"How?" says Shalini.

"By bombarding her with smiles," I say. "A person who is smiled at has to smile back eventually. It's like a yawn. If I yawn, you'll yawn." I yawn a huge yawn, with an added stretch of the arms to prove my point. They both join in and my point is proved.

"I shall name it *Plan A: The Train Ms Thorn To Smile So That I Am Not Intimidated By Her Looks Plan*."

"It might help if you make her happy too," says Jess. "Happy people smile."

"Yes, but what makes her happy?"

"Rules," says Shalini. "She loves rules."

"But you got rid of those when you inherited the school after you deceased your Greats-Grandma Ursula," says Jess. She aims the blower at her tights.

"Ooooh, I know." Her eyes light up as if she's had another idea of genius. "Dominique makes her happy," she says. "You must *Be More Dominique*!"

Urgh. The thought of being even a tiny bit Dominique makes me feel queasy. But it is true. Dominique is like a Ms Thorn clone and Ms Thorn does give her extra ticks, which is really not fair. I ponder on that as we move to the next cubicle.

Suddenly something drops down on to my hat with a thump and I think, *Oh dungpats, not another one.* This is beginning to get annoying!

3

Summary:

A statue has dropped on to my head. A little one. Not enough to hurt. It's a statue of me. Someone, or something, is ac-chew-ally leaving tiny statues of me all over school. They're like the marble ones in the West Wing, only small. It's embarrassing. Like having a stalker fan. Dominique and Arwen think I'm making them to show off. I'm not.

Jess picks the statue off the brim of my hat.

"Oh, this one's brilliant," she says. "Look." She holds it out. A mini me is standing on her outstretched palm. "You have your hands on your hips and you're doing a look from *The Book of Annoyed*. It's so cute. Can I keep it?"

"You can keep them all," I say crossly. "You can decorate your cauldron with them. You can fill up your cauldron cupboard with them if you like."

"You can't possibly fill up a cauldron cupboard," says Shalini. "It's impossible. It'll just grow to—"

"Fit whatever's in there. I know that," I say. "I do ac-chew-ally sleep in one."

"You don't sleep in a cauldron cupboard," says Jess. "You sleep in a—"

"Cauldron! I know."

There is a hint, possibly more, of crossness in my reply because I am in an emotional turmoil and being precise about cauldrons and cupboards when I am in an emotional turmoil is impossible.

The reason for my emotional turmoil is this – even though I have *Plan A*, which is a plan of genius, I have just had a panic-creating thought which is slightly different to my other, earlier, worrying thoughts.

This thought is – *If I don't get to perform my Bottom in an ac-chew-al theatre tonight it might be my last chance to perform anything – EVER.*

Because...

What if this is Mr Marlow's very last performance of A Midsummer Night's Dream *and he starts rehearsing another play and I can't be in it?*

Because...

I am not a pupil at St Bluebottle's School of Creativity and Fun. I am a pupil at Toadspit Towers, Witch School of Conformity and Strictness.

I decide to ban all future worrying thoughts! I shall keep my brain totally thoughtless until it stops thinking bad things.

A bell rings. Oh dungpats.

"Oh no!" says Shalini.

"Breakfast time!" says Jess. "And we're on the top floor!" She starts to run. We follow.

I limp. My toes hurt. I think my boots have shrunk with the wetting and then the drying. I ignore the pain because Ms Thorn has a new rule. Anyone late for lessons or meals has two whole ticks, for each five minutes of lateness, removed from the Boards of Embarrassment in the dining hall. The boards that

show how many ticks each person has earned in a day, a week, a month, a year. Having your report on the wall for everyone to see every single day is NOT a good thing.

I run-limp. I must not lose ticks! Ticks mean pies!

"Last one there eats gloop!" shouts Jess.

"Ms Sage said to mind the walls," shouts Shalini from behind me as I bump into one and there's a shower of granite dust. "You know the school is falling to bits!"

"It isn't my fault," I shout back. This may not be tech-nic-ally true.

"I didn't say it was," says Shalini. She overtakes me.

We race down flights of rickety stairs and along landings that threaten to trip us up with frayed carpets and uneven floorboards.

We are not first to arrive at the dining hall but we're not last either. We queue up to pay our respects to the witchwood roots entwined around the double doors. Nearly everyone in front of us has been running too,

25

they're red-faced and panting. When it's our turn Jess goes first, then Shalini, then me.

This is one of my favourite moments of the day. I touch the Celtic patterns of twisted roots and a fizzingle fizzes through my fingers. I am the only one the witchwood tree fizzingles because I am the only witch descended from Greats-Grandma Ursula who founded the school and planted the tree. Plus, I am the bearer of the tree charm and I am part-witchwood – my thumb – so I have a very special magical bond with the tree. It likes me.

A fizzingle is the best feeling in the whole world of feelings. It's like being flooded with fizzy lemonade but without the threat of burps. I am always reluctant to let go but I can't live my life attached to a tree and there is the promise of delicious food for breakfast so I say, "I give thanks to the witchwood," and pull my hand away.

It won't come. My witchwood thumb has attached itself to the Celtic knots with tiny threads of witchwood.

"Blimey," says Jess, inspecting my thumb and the connection. "That doesn't usually happen."

Shalini's doing the curious-eyebrow look. Her left eyebrow is always the one to lift. The other is usually hidden under the floppy brim of her hat. So tech-nic-ally she could be lifting both and I would not know. "Curious," she says.

I pull and the root threads make tiny snapping sounds as my thumb is released. My thumb feels odd, like a prickly fizz has been left inside, just under the nail. I try to shake the feeling away as we enter the hall.

There are witchwood cats dozing in the roots around the walls. Oddbod's there. He sees me and jumps down. He saunters towards us doing the walk of *Cat Who Owns The Room*. He's more cat than kitten now. He's growing fast. Maybe too fast.

Shalini loves the whole witchwood cat born-again thing but I am dreading Oddbod's regeneration. What if he turns to cat-ash and we don't find his pile of cat-ash in time to return him to the witchwood? What if he doesn't regenerate?

Oddbod rubs his head on my boot. He's sniffing my leg.

What if he forgets me? I shall be witchwood cat-less. I put that thought away because it is another bad thought and I must focus on the *Train Ms Thorn To Smile Plan*. That has priority.

Ms Thorn is at the teachers' dining table. She is not dining. She is watching everyone enter and she's glancing at the grandfather clock at the back of the stage. We must have run fast. There's five minutes to go before time's up and ticks are taken. Success! Our ticks are safe.

Ms Thorn is a very straight person. It's as if she doesn't allow her joints to bend without permission. She's taken to wearing the same suit every day now that she's deputy headmistress. A red one with a high collar holding her chin up. It's like her very own school uniform. Fangus is clinging on to her hat, wings spread wide. The black bat on the red hat looks like a warning: Do Not Approach. So I Don't.

Dominique and Arwen are already at our table. They look disappointed to see us. I suspect they were hoping we would lose ticks.

Ms Thorn glances at us. I put Plan A into operation. The training shall begin! I smile a smile with just the right amount of smile. Not so wide it could be considered overenthusiastic. Not so small as to be confused with a sneer. I hold it in place and whisper to my friends out of the corner of my mouth, "We should sit down immediately to show we are Pupils of Perfection."

I attempt to walk a walk of *Watch Me Being Obedient* but my boots are pinching even more and it turns into a walk of *Ouch*. Ms Thorn looks away because more girls have arrived.

Jess gasps and grabs my hand. It's the type of gasp that's always followed by an "uh-oh". It is my least favourite of all of the gasps.

"Uh-oh," she says, as predicted. "Look at your thumb!" She's holding up my thumb. "This doesn't usually happen either."

She's right. I can't help it. I gasp too. So does Shalini. My thumbnail is ac-chew-ally growing. It's growing and twisting into a witchwood root. It's making a knot, like the knots around the door.

Oh warty boils and pimples!

This is a TRAGEDY!

I think I am ac-chew-ally turning into A TREE!

30

4

Summary:

This is a DISASTER! How can I act my Bottom if I turn into a tree! How can I act a WALL if I turn into a tree! If I turn into a tree the only thing I will ever be able to act will be – A TREE!

I briefly wonder if this will make Ms Thorn smile. This is unlikely.

We stop walking. We make a circle. We inspect my thumb-twig. Oddbod is trying to climb up my leg.

"Does it hurt?" says Shalini. She touches it with her fingertip as if she'll feel any hurt through her fingers. "Can you feel it growing?"

"It's prickling."

Jess studies it. "Oooh, look."

It's growing a bud. I shake my hand in the hope it will STOP GROWING! It doesn't. I act not panicking but then I think *Why am I not panicking?! Panicking is completely justified. Panicking is exactly what I should be doing.* So I do panic.

I grab Jess. I hiss-whisper loudly into her face. "What am I going to do? What if the tree takes over until I am mostly tree?! What if it takes over until I am ALL TREE?!"

Some of the girls turn around.

"Calm down, Twink," says Shalini.

"Calm down!" I can't believe she's said that to a person turning into a tree. "Shalini! Look!"

"I know," she says, holding her hand under the twig that is now three times longer than my thumb should be. "But I saw Ms Thorn's leg grow a twig once and she hasn't turned into a tree."

"Hasn't she?" says Jess, glancing over at the teacher. "It could explain how straight she is."

"And the lack of emotion." I say this with horror. "Maybe her heart has turned to wood! Maybe I will ac-chew-ally turn into a Ms Thorn! I shall be EMOTIONLESS!"

"Stop it," says Shalini. "Both of you," she adds, as Jess is about to say something else. "We should go and see the expert on all things growing. Ms Lobelia. Plus, she has a witchwood finger—"

"Her little finger," says Jess. She waves her little finger on the left.

"—so she should be able to help. Perhaps it's normal."

I give Shalini a look from *The Book of WHAT?!*

"For people with witchwood bits," she says. "Like Ms Lobelia and Ms Thorn."

Ms Thorn does not have a witchwood *bit*. Her entire left leg is all witchwood. My thumb was bitten off by a couple of nasty little scarabites and that was PAINFUL. I would definitely not like to have a WHOLE LEG bitten off.

"Maybe it just needs pruning," says Jess.

I hide my hand inside my shirt and we walk through the tables, towards the Garden of Doom. Oddbod is by my side. He's meowing. I think he's trying to reassure me. It's not working.

I am now doing the *Walk of Hurrying While Pretending Not To Hurry* and I daren't turn round to see if Ms Thorn is watching because becoming a tree may come under *disrupting the school*. Dominique and Arwen are watching, though. They're both doing the curious-eyebrow look.

My cheeks feel red. I am flushed. I feel like all eyes are on me. I check. They're not. The girls are watching the Boards of Embarrassment, waiting for the tick updates and the new comments.

Maybe the witchwood dolls that line the wall opposite the Boards of Embarrassment are watching me? Can they? Are they following me with their tiny dead eyes? They're not moving. I move. We reach the French doors, they're open.

I hear Ms Lobelia singing before I see her. It's not difficult to hear Ms Lobelia. Her voice is as big as she is. She's stacking cauldrons. Five high. They're wobbly. She starts a new song just as we get there.

"Oh, the jolly witch of Googleheim, she had a hairy nose, and every time she blew it, the hairy hairs did groooow…"

I suspect Ms Lobelia is part garden. Her hair is a bush, her hat is a trellis of ivy leaves, and her jacket and trousers are always covered with splodges of pollen. The splodges are purple today from the giant purple flower in her lapel. It's big like a chrysanthemum with stamens that curl and uncurl. I don't trust it. The smell is yucky, like mouldy cheese.

Sniffler, her Toadspit creature, is jumping about in a tree that has dark-red curly leaves, like fingers. The leaves are trying to catch him and failing. He chitters at us and dances on the branch. Then suddenly he's caught. He squeaks and wriggles.

"Oh no!" says Jess. She aims her spoon and sings the deep "*Eeeeeowww*" of the weedkiller note. The leaves let go and the tree shudders from top to bottom.

Ms Lobelia stops singing. "Oh, my goodness, Jessica! Stop! You'll ruin the blooms," she booms. She strokes the tree trunk. "Shhhhhhhh," she murmurs. "Shhhhh." The tree stops shaking and Ms Lobelia relaxes.

"We never use the weedkiller note unless it's an absolute emergency, Jessica. A life and death situation. A no-other-choice scenario. Sniffler was in no danger from the redwillow. Watch."

Sniffler allows himself to be caught and tickled by the leafy fingers. He escapes and then gets caught again. His squeaks are funny.

"So," says Ms Lobelia, turning back to us. "Have you all come to volunteer to plant the boggleweeds after breakfast?" She takes a trowel out of her tool belt and waves it at a line of plant pots. "The seedlings are ready but you will need a pair of sturdy gloves each."

The plants turn their long spiky leaves towards us. As if they're listening for the answer.

"No, Ms Lobelia," says Shalini. "Twink has a problem."

Jess holds up my thumb. "We think she needs pruning," she says.

"Oh," says Ms Lobelia. "How wonderful!" She says this with a rather big smile. Personally, I think it's a bit of an odd response to the fact that I am growing a BRANCH!

She puts the trowel back in her belt and pulls me over to her deckchair. It's blue and white stripes. Or it was. The colours have either faded in the sun or worn away from her bottom.

"Sit," she says. I sit. Oddbod jumps on to my knee. He licks my thumb; it tingles. Jess and Shalini stand behind me and peer over the top of my head as Ms Lobelia takes a large magnifying glass from her top pocket.

"I've been waiting for this," she says. She inspects my thumb from every angle. "Has anything else grown?" I must be looking puzzled. "Clothes too tight? Shirt collar rubbing? Boots don't fit?"

"Boots," I say. "My boots are tight. I thought it was because they got wet."

She shakes her head. "You're having a growth spurt, Twinkle, and you share witchwood DNA. So because *you're* growing, *it's* growing." She returns the magnifying glass to her pocket.

"So I'm not going to turn into a tree?" I am hopeful she will say no.

She laughs and gives me one of her giant squishy hugs. Oddbod is squashed between us. He meows a complaint and she lets go. "Of course not. No. You just have to learn how to control it. Show it who's boss. That should be easy for our one and only seventh of seven witch!" She laughs her booming, cheerful laugh.

I do not laugh. Her expectations regarding my unknown potential are far too high.

"Off you go," she says to Shalini and Jess. "Go and have your breakfast. I've got this." My friends are reluctant. She shoos them away.

"Good luck," says Shalini.

Jess gives my shoulder a squeeze. "You can do this," she says. They leave.

"What do I do?" I say to Ms Lobelia.

"You just have to think it back to normal," she says.

I don't think the word JUST is appropriate. Thinking your thumb back to normal is not a normal thing to JUST do. I must be doing a look from *The Book of Not Liking That Solution* because she gives me another big squishy hug. I suffocate briefly. She lets go.

"Don't worry," she says. "The cure is simple. Take a deep breath. Close your eyes and imagine your thumb, as it is now, in your zen space. See the witchwood atoms. See the space between them. Think the space smaller."

I repeat that. "Think the space smaller?" She nods, as if this makes perfect sense.

Not turning into a tree is becoming URGENT.

My thumbnail tree-twig is turning into a thumbnail tree-branch. It's dragging my hand off my knee and down towards the floor. It's heavy. I must follow Ms Lobelia's instructions. NOW. I hug Oddbod with my free hand and close my eyes. I empty my mind. I add a picture of my current witchwood thumb to my zen space. It fills it.

"Do you have the picture?" says Ms Lobelia.

I do. I nod.

"Good. Now. Look at the atoms."

I do.

"Look at the spaces."

I do.

"Think them small."

How?! I think the word *small*. I think the word *tiny*. I think the word *minute*. I feel my thumbnail tree-branch touch the floor. I think of small things, like poppy seeds and pinheads. Nothing works!

"Hmm," says Ms Lobelia. "Maybe a rhyme will help. It's best if you use one of your own. Maybe something with shrink in. Or shrivel. Or decrease. Or diminish. Contract, compress or waste away?"

They're all good words, especially shrivel, but my mind is full of tree and I can't think of a single rhyme and I am wishing Ms Lobelia was Ms Thorn because Ms Thorn would have TOLD me which rhyme to use and would not expect me to MAKE ONE UP. I am beginning to think panicky thoughts about FAILING and turning into a FOREST!

"Try something like this," says Ms Lobelia.

"Witchwood, witchwood, hear my plea, take a look at my thumb for me. It's so big you must agree …"

"… I don't want to be a TREE," I say with feeling.

"Excellent, now do one of your own. This is between you and your witchwood."

I try. "Witchwood thumb, please hear my plea … I don't want to be a tree…" I think of the words Ms Lobelia suggested. "Shrink and shrivel … waste away … be the thumb of yesterday!"

I feel my thumbnail tree-branch shudder. I feel pins and needles in my hand.

"Excellent!" says Ms Lobelia. "The rhyme's the solution! Say it again."

"Witchwood thumb, please hear my plea, I don't want to be a tree. Shrink and shrivel, waste away, be the thumb of yesterday!"

"Oh, well done, Twinkle!" says Ms Lobelia. "You've got the hang of it. Keep rhyming."

I can feel it shrinking. The pins and needles run up my arm. I keep my arm absolutely still because pins and needles HURT if you move. I say the rhyme faster

and faster and faster until the words are garbled and mashed together but I don't care because I open my eyes and my thumb is a thumb. There is an absence of leaf, twig and branch and I am IN CONTROL!

Ms Lobelia claps her hands. "Oh, well done, you little twinkling star! It should stabilise over the next few weeks," she says. "Just keep training it and you'll be fine."

"Training it?"

"Of course, Twinkle. Every time you have a growth spurt, the witchwood will have a growth spurt. You just have to train it to have a small one. And avoid any stress for a few weeks. Stress can be a huge trigger."

What?! I have a sudden thought even though, as previously mentioned, I have banned thoughts. It is not a good thought. It is a thought beyond panic. It is a thought of TERROR! The thought is this...

5

Summary of my thought:

What if a tree branch grows out of my thumb while I'm on stage in front of Ms Thorn? THAT is a STRESSFUL situation! What will I do then? It would be a DISASTER!

I go back to the dining hall with Oddbod and I think of this and nothing but this until I spot the Boards of Embarrassment. They have clicked. I have lost four ticks! They've gone down to sixteen. Why have they gone down? This means I only have enough left for four pies or eight sausages or sixteen slices of toast. I calculate I only have two days of food left before I will be forced to eat GLOOP for breakfast, dinner and tea. I could be wrong. I'm an actress, not a mathematician.

Ms Thorn is watching me. She looks at the clock and then back at me then at a new board. It's black. It says at the top – RULES. There is only one rule, so far.

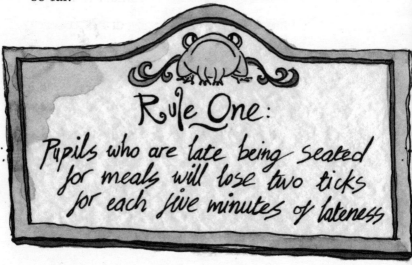

Rule One:
Pupils who are late being seated for meals will lose two ticks for each five minutes of lateness

This is so not fair! That rule was not there when we arrived. She's added the being seated bit. I want to go over to her and demand that she puts my ticks back but instead I take a deep breath and walk a *Walk of Obedience* to our table and keep to the plan. I smile, but not a wide one, and wave, but not enthusiastically.

I act apologetic for being late. She does not smile back. I wave my thumb hand at Jess and Shalini too so they can see I am cured, temporarily. Oddbod spots a mouse and leaves me to go mouse chasing.

My mood lightens as I see my breakfast is already on the table. I have ordered one sticky, dribbly cherry pie of deliciousness because pie for breakfast is the BEST way to start the day.

Unfortunately, there is another mini statue by my plate. This darkens my mood. I sigh. I am on a rollercoaster of emotional moods and this does not bode well for a stress-free day. My mood darkens even further when Arwen speaks.

She's obviously been desperate for me to arrive so she can annoy me about the statue. "I see you have created another Twinkle Toadspit likeness," she says, as I sit down. "It really is sad, having to be your own fan."

I do not respond. Instead, I cut into my pie and focus on the steam that steams from the bubbly red fruit inside. It's too hot to eat. A piece of pastry falls off, I pick it up and blow on it. I do not wish to answer Arwen immediately because Arwen is doing her best to goad me into trouble and I am doing my best *not* to be goaded into trouble because, as previously stated, I am currently a Pupil of Perfection and cannot be goaded into anything. Especially when Ms Thorn is watching. Which she is.

I nibble the piece of pastry; the edge is cherry flavoured deliciousness. It calms me. I sigh with contentment. I am under control and have an answer.

"Arwen, oh, fairest Arwen. I wish you were correct. I wish my magical creativity was powerful enough to create such tiny works of art but I'm afraid it isn't. I know it's difficult but you will just have to accept that I have an ac-chew-al fan."

"A secret admirer," says Jess. She takes the statue and undoes the button on her pocket of usefulness. It sucks in the statue.

"A very talented secret admirer," says Shalini.

Dominique watches the statue disappear, pretending not to. Arwen shrugs. "So you say," she

says, which is one of those things that people say that can be very annoying. Like *Of course it is* and *I believe you* and *I said you were right* when they mean the complete opposite and they are just trying to wind you up. She does not need to wind me up. I am already wound up.

She concentrates on eating her toast. I pretend to concentrate on my still-cooling pie but, secretly, I am checking my thumb. There is no change.

I also secretly study Ms Thorn. She's currently behaving like a human statue, one that can only move its head. I suspect she is inspecting the room for conformity and compliance. Ms Lobelia has joined the teachers. She's laughing. The others are laughing. Ms Thorn is not. There is no hint of smile even though Ms Lobelia is the expert at making people smile.

My pie has cooled so I take a big bite. It is DELICIOUS! Perhaps Ms Thorn needs to eat more pie because cherry pie equals happiness. Perhaps I should offer her some? I don't. I take another bite

and continue to secretly study.

Ms Thorn hardly reacts when Ms Sage arrives, just a brief nod of acknowledgement. I suspect Ms Sage does not make Ms Thorn happy either.

"Does anyone else think Ms Sage is looking a bit frazzled round the edges?" says Jess. She's finished her blueberry yoghurt and she's wiping the bowl with her last piece of toast to make sure she gets every drop.

Dominique tsks. *Tsk.* As if this is not acceptable behaviour.

Ms Sage's hat is definitely frazzled. The golden velvet looks rough, as if someone has rubbed it up the wrong way, and the swirls of fabric and ribbon are floppy. There's even a strand of golden lace dangling loose at the back and she looks as if she's slept in her dress. The velvet is crumpled and the yellow is dull. Even the silver stars are refusing to twinkle.

Shalini nods in agreement with Jess. "I'm not sure being the new headmistress of Toadspit Towers is as easy as she thought it would be," she says.

"Ms Sage was a perfectly good *deputy* headmistress," says Dominique. "It was a disaster for the school when you arrived," she is looking directly at me, "and deceased Ms Ursula Toadspit forcing Ms Sage to take over. You are to blame for Ms Sage's difficulties."

She is so unfair! Ms Sage did not need forcing. Ms Sage was desperate to be headmistress.

"Dominique," I say, in a voice of calm firmness, "I would like to remind you that it was not my fault that I was dumped at Toadspit Towers."

"That was Granny Wart's fault," says Jess.

"And it was not my fault that my Greats-Grandma Ursula Toadspit's ghostly headmistress doll was waiting for a Toadspit to arrive and take over. Waiting for a Toadspit to break the Toadspit curse so she could die properly."

"That was Greats-Grandma Marietta Toadspit's fault," says Jess.

I glance up at my Greats-Grandma Ursula's doll at the top of the doll display. It hasn't moved since

Ms Thorn placed it there. It has not whizzed into a Toadspit Tornado of greenness, making sure the rules are kept and nothing is changed. It is a dead doll. The same as all the others.

Jess says, "None of it was Twink's fault because she didn't know she was a Toadspit. She didn't know she was breaking the curse because she thought she was a Wart, like her granny. So you can't blame her for any unexpected consequences."

Arwen almost falls off her chair laughing. "She thought she was a Wart! You were a wart! Now you're..." She's struggling to find another insult.

I help. "A witch of mega power who will own the school one day?"

She laughs even more. "Mega power? You only have sixteen ticks!" she says. "Dominique earned a hundred and fifty last week so she's the witch of mega power, not you."

Dominique smirks a tiny smirk as if she's too important to bother with a big smirk. She's at the top of the red-hats board and her picture is back in the Best and Brightest golden frame. She will do *anything* to prove she is the B&B of all time.

I do not answer Arwen. She is *not* winding me up. I am in control of my emotions. I act not bothered. I stare at what's left of my pie. A few sticky lumps of cherry and crusts of pastry. I think of pie and nothing but pie. I eat but the deliciousness isn't quite as delicious as it was.

Arwen will not stop goading me.

"*You* released the evil Jacobus charm from the secret tower room, Wrinkle," she says. "You endangered the school." She is ac-chew-ally stabbing her finger towards me.

Dominique joins in. "Arwen is correct. Your reckless behaviour endangers the school. You should not be allowed to investigate any more secret rooms. You should leave that to the true Best and Brightest of Toadspit Towers." She looks meaningfully at her picture in the Best and Brightest golden frame then back at me. "You should be supervised at all times because you are still *ignorant*."

Aargh! She's used the *I* word! This is definitely becoming a potentially stressful situation! I act deaf as Arwen and Dominique continue to list my failures. Jess and Shalini defend me as I attempt to block them out by concentrating on something else. I can't concentrate on pie because there is no pie left so I undo my pocket of usefulness button, stick my hand in and say, "Fetch Shakespeare." *The Complete History of William Shakespeare*, with pictures, is immediately in my hand. I pull it out and it grows to the right size. It falls open on the table at *A Midsummer Night's Dream*.

I try to rehearse the words but Arwen's voice is the sort of voice that pierces a person's mind like a stabbing pin so I stare at the pictures instead.

Oberon, the fairy king, is squeezing the juice from a little purple pansy flower on to Titania's sleeping eyelids. It will make the fairy queen love the first person she sees when she wakes. I have an idea of genius! I should give Arwen a love potion! Or maybe just a *like* potion. That would shut her up.

Ms Sage interrupts my thoughts. She's on the stage. Horatio flies off her charm bracelet and on to her shoulder. He hoots for silence. The girls shush but I can still hear the scraping of cutlery on china as they finish their meals.

"Good morning, girls," says Ms Sage.

The girls answer, "Good morning, Ms Sage." I do too.

"I'm afraid I have to tell you that Ms Rowanstall has reported on the ongoing Crumbling Building Situation and it is not good news. The unfortunate removal of Ms Ursula Toadspit's angelica protection from the walls of Toadspit Towers and the sudden replacement of the angelica protection back into the walls has caused the building to become dangerously

55

unstable and it could fall down at any moment."

We all look up as if *this* is that moment. It isn't.

"Ms Rowanstall and the maintenance team have been working overtime to solve the problem but this is a rather large school and therefore rather a large problem."

"That is definitely your fault," hiss-whispers Arwen. "You broke the Gellica Charm of Protection."

This is tech-nic-ally true but I also put it back together again and she's not mentioning that.

"You must all do your part to assist the maintenance team. You must not touch the walls, lean on the walls, draw on the walls or even look at the walls. And definitely No Ball Games. Failure to obey this instruction could be catastrophic. If a pupil is injured, crushed or squashed the school may have to CLOSE! Therefore all lessons are cancelled and everyone will be trained in maintenance techniques. If we all work together we may just be able to save Toadspit Towers from TOTAL DESTRUCTION!"

She puts her hand on her heart and steps back. Ms

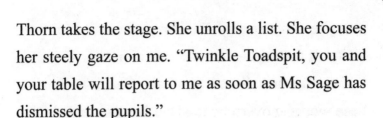

Thorn takes the stage. She unrolls a list. She focuses her steely gaze on me. "Twinkle Toadspit, you and your table will report to me as soon as Ms Sage has dismissed the pupils."

I immediately stand to demonstrate compliance and say, "Yes, Ms Thorn. Of course, Ms Thorn," although I really want to say, *What about the seats? Why just the table?* But I suspect Ms Thorn will consider that insubordination or cheek so I desist and sit back down.

Ms Thorn reads to the bottom of the list, matching up the other girls with their teachers and tasks. As soon as she's finished, Dominique and Arwen leap to their feet as if it's essential that they get to Ms Thorn first, to prove they are better and keener witches than we are.

I consider hurrying so that I arrive before them but I don't. I close my book, touch it to my pocket and it shrinks in. Then I stand. I do *The Walk of Sensibleness*. This involves acting. Jess and Shalini copy.

Ms Thorn is waiting. She's leaning forward. Resting on her cane. She glances at my thumb. I hope Ms Lobelia has not told her about the tree! Why didn't I swear Ms Lobelia to secrecy? Although, maybe it's a good thing if she knows. Maybe we can bond over our witchwood bits. Laugh about our witchwood's quirks? I am hopeful.

Ms Thorn continues to look at me. She's inspecting me. Assessing me. Judging me. I smile. She does not. Dominique steps between us.

"What would you like I to do, Ms Thorn?" she says.

Ms Thorn replies. "Follow me." She walks away.

Thunk, tap, thunk, tap, thunk, tap goes her witchwood cane and her witchwood leg on the flagstones.

We follow. Dominique and Arwen first. Then Shalini, me and Jess.

Shalini's muttering under her breath. "But what about the toilets? We haven't finished the toilets. We should really finish the toilets."

We leave by the door on the right of the stage and

follow Ms Thorn through unknown corridors that soon become even shabbier and dustier than the corridors we normally walk through. After a while I glance behind. We are leaving footprints. The portraits on the walls are dull, the witches' faces dark and murky with a thick layer of dust.

Ms Thorn doesn't talk as she leads us lefts and rights, along dark corridors and down a creaky wooden staircase. The dark becomes darker at the bottom. We brighten our hat-lights.

I don't talk either because, as previously mentioned, I am currently the Pupil of Perfection. A Queen of Compliance and Obedience.

Jess is not.

"Where are we?" she says. "Where are we going?" she says. "Where are we?" she says again.

Ms Thorn does not answer. This does not stop Jess.

"What are we looking for? Are we in the East Wing? What's in the East Wing? Can we even get in the East Wing?"

I do not answer either. Not just because I do not

know the answer, but because I suspect Ms Thorn requires silence and Ms Thorn must be kept happy. Ms Thorn must be obeyed. Ms Thorn must be – on my side.

The corridor opens out into a room, like an entrance hall. There are no windows or doors, just a stone archway straight ahead carved with roses and leaves. It's totally blocked by chunks of granite spilling out like a frozen waterfall of rock.

This bit of the school has ac-chew-ally fallen down already! It does not fill me full of hope for the rest of the school. There are no paintings on the walls here. The floor is not just dusty, it's full of stones and grit and there's a complete absence of light apart from our hat-lights. They're casting shadows of gloom on our faces. I name Dominique *Doominique La'Spooky* and Arwen *Arwen De'Ghoul*.

"This," says Ms Thorn, pointing at the blockage then me, "is your new task."

Shalini's toilet frustration gushes over. "But what about the toilets, Ms Thorn? We have to do the toilets

all in one day or the hex will spread."

"Another group will be assigned that task, Shalini."

This does not seem to please Shalini but I act just the right amount of enthusiasm and say, with a smile of positivity, "Jolly good. Let's get started," because the clock is ticking towards the rehearsal this afternoon and that's a BIG BLOCKAGE and I am running out of time to make Ms Thorn smile.

Ms Thorn directs her words at me again. "I shall train you in the necessary techniques to repair the granite and you will assist me in unblocking the entrance."

Entrance to what? I'm thinking.

"Entrance to what?" says Jess, like a mind reader.

"To the East Wing," says Ms Thorn.

"I knew it," says Jess.

"The East Wing?" says Shalini. "But hasn't that been—"

"Magically locked for hundreds of years," says Jess.

6

"You are correct, Jessica," says Ms Thorn. "Ms Toadspit placed a charm on the East Wing, preventing access to all. However, now that Twinkle's arrival has caused all of Ms Toadspit's protective charms to become unstable it is possible the East Wing's protections have broken too and this could be disastrous for the school. Those protections must be assessed. I have taken on that task. Once the corridor has been repaired I shall enter the wing and conduct a survey. Twinkle shall accompany me as it is *possible* she may be useful in repairing her ancestor's protections."

She doesn't sound like she believes the last bit. Plus she's talking about me as if I am not here. As if I'm just a tool in her toolkit. Which is annoying but I refuse to be annoyed so I act smiling a Smile of Sincerity and say, "I am happy to be of service, Ms Thorn, and I shall obey your every command. The school shall be saved!" I increase the size of the smile and attempt to add a twinkle to my eyes. Surely this will get me one back!

It does not. She doesn't even give me a look from *The Book of Thanks For The Obedience* so I follow my comment with, "What wouldst thou have me do before the morning is over, Ms Thorn?" to show willingness and to remind her I am a Shakespearean actress with a rehearsal to attend in the afternoon.

"You must follow my instructions," she says. "To the letter. Exactly. Precisely. No creativity. No inventiveness. No original ideas are required. Just compliance." She taps her cane on the floor with each instruction. Fangus has his beady little eyes on me. Maybe I should train him to smile too.

"I shall comply with thee, Ms Thorn," I say. "I implore thee to instruct me in the instructions that must be obeyed and I shall obey them."

Dominique tsks. *Tsk.* Arwen rolls her eyes.

Ms Thorn does not react but then I spot a tiny twitch. It is a twitch of annoyance in her eyebrow. The twitch is in the wrong place! It should be a twitch of amusement on the lips. I have a bad thought. Maybe she is allergic to smiling. Or maybe she's just allergic to *my* smiles. Maybe I should keep a list of other things that make her happy. Things that work and things that don't work. Things that have *not* worked so far: enthusiasm, willingness, humour, friendliness. Things that *have* worked so far: nothing.

"Step one," says Ms Thorn. "You must remove all of the loose granite. Care must be taken not to dislodge a supporting block that could potentially cause a further slide. I do not wish to bring the ceiling down."

She looks at me as she says that. I think she has trust issues.

"Dominique, you shall be responsible for removing the loose granite."

Dominique is thrilled to have been singled out for

a special job that involves the word *responsible*.

"You may demonstrate this skill," says Ms Thorn.

She steps back. Dominique steps forward. She aims her spoon, stares at the blockage, crosses her eyes and a few seconds later a lump of granite falls away. It bounces towards me. I dodge it. She uncrosses her eyes and aims a superior smirk in my direction.

"Excellent work," says Ms Thorn. There is a twitch of the lip! A hint of a smile.

So it is possible! Maybe Jess is right. I must *Be More Dominique*. This is Plan Z.

"I shall award you one tick," says the teacher. She draws the tick in the air with her pointy red fingernail. The tick appears like a tick-shaped sparkler in the darkness then fizzles out.

Dominique does her look from *The Book of Superior Looks* and Arwen copies. Ms Thorn continues with the task.

"Step two: You will each create new blocks by joining the broken pieces."

"Like a jigsaw," I say. I act an intelligent look.

Head on the side, nodding slightly. Dominique rolls more granite chunks my way.

"That is incorrect," says Ms Thorn. "We are not reconnecting previously broken pieces. We are bringing together pieces at random. Magically."

"With magic glue," I say, with another nod of intelligence.

"No," says Ms Thorn. I suspect intelligent looks and helpful suggestions are *not* the key to Ms Thorn's smile. I try once more, to confirm my suspicion.

"With magic sticky tape?" I say.

"No," she says.

I have confirmed it – intelligence has a negative effect. I cease and desist. She is such a tough audience! I act patience as Dominique rolls another chunk my way. Soon we all have enough to get started.

Ms Thorn instructs us. "Unhook your spoons." We obey.

"Step one: You will choose enough granite to create a new block."

I ponder on how I should be acting as Ms Thorn

tells us what to do. Observant? Obedient? Interested? I go with *Fascinated*.

"Step three."

Dungpats! I've missed step two! What did she say for step two? She has her eyes crossed so I'm guessing – cross your eyes.

"You will visualise the atoms coming together into a whole block of granite. Step four: You will aim your spoon and say this rhyme and only this rhyme. *Granite separate, split and cracked, atoms pulling must attract. Granite broken, granite whole, I bind the atoms with control.*"

We all repeat the spell. She makes us say it again and again until she's satisfied. She takes a step back. "Begin," she says.

This is my chance to impress her. So I move Plan Z up to Plan A and decide to *Be More Dominique*. But just for this task. I watch what Dominique does. She chooses three odd-shaped blocks of granite. I do the same. She inspects them, rearranges them. I do the same. The broken sides twinkle with tiny little pink and white twinkles, like tiny stars embedded in the rock. She aims her spoon at the stones and crosses her eyes. I start to do the same.

But as I aim my spoon and cross my eyes I feel a pricking in my thumb. Oh, warty boils! Not now! I uncross my eyes. My thumbnail is growing! It's twisting into a knot. Curling around itself. This is terrible timing!

I wasn't even stressed but now…

I AM EXTREMELY STRESSED!

7

Summary:

I must not be stressed! I am panicking. I am panicking about being stressed which is increasing the stress! What if Ms Thorn sees? What if she says I can't leave Toadspit Towers until I can control my thumb! All plans will have failed!

I turn away. I must control the witchwood before it becomes a twig! Before it becomes a branch! I close my eyes, throw out the images of granite that have filled my zen space and visualise my thumb as I want it to be. I repeat my shrivelling rhyme under my breath. I mumble it, I think it, I imagine it and soon I feel painful pins and needles in my hand and my arm.

I open my eyes.

Success! My thumb is back to normal. And failure! Everyone has a shiny pink, white and grey granite block, except me. I still have a pile of rubble. A very small pile of rubble.

Ms Thorn has a hint of a frown on her face and it's directed at me.

"I thought I had made myself clear," she says. "There is to be NO creativity. NO inventiveness. NO original ideas. Whatever you were muttering was incorrect."

This is so unfair! I want to argue. I want to say, "But I just controlled the witchwood and stopped myself turning into a tree! You should be impressed!" But I don't want her to know about my current thumb situation, so I bite the words back and I act sorry even though I am not sorry. It ac-chew-ally occurs to me that I do more acting in real life than I do on the stage!

I act calm and say, "I am sorry I failed you, Ms Thorn. Please may I try again?"

"You must," says Ms Thorn, but before I can begin there's a whoosh over my head and I duck, thinking the ceiling is ac-chew-ally falling down on our heads, as suggested earlier, and I'm about to be crushed. It isn't. It's Horatio gliding above me towards Ms Thorn. She holds her arm out and he lands. His talons press into the fabric of her red suit. She raises him to her ear and listens. She frowns. A proper one. This is not hint of a frown. It's a both-eyebrows-down frown.

"Ms Sage urgently requires my assistance," she says. Horatio flies off. Fangus whooshes off her hat, spins into a charm and attaches himself to her

bracelet. "You shall all remain here and complete your task. Dominique, you will take charge."

Dominique immediately sends a smirk in my direction. I ignore it.

This is a DISASTER with dire consequences for my acting career! How can I train Ms Thorn in the art of smiling if she isn't here? How can she bond with me emotionally if we are on opposite sides of the school? I have a solution. I shall offer my assistance.

"Ms Thorn. I offer you my assistance in whatever task Ms Sage requires help with."

"That will not be necessary, Twinkle," she says. There is an absence of *Thank you for offering*. She keeps on talking. "You will all mark the stones you have created with your initials. I shall test each block on my return. There shall be one tick for each successfully transformed stone. There shall be five ticks for the person who has created the most blocks. Comply and conform with my instructions. I will know if any other spell is used. Should you clear a way through, you will report to me immediately."

She stands in front of me. I look up. She looks down. "You will not enter the East Wing. You will not feel the need to explore."

I attempt to reassure her, maybe reassurance is the key to our emotional bonding. "Ms Thorn, I can assure you I have no interest in exploring the East Wing. I have absolutely no time for exploring. As you are aware, I have a performance to prepare for." I add that as a reminder that she must keep her side of the deal. "We need to leave at one o'clock for the rehearsal and I really want you to enjoy tonight's performance."

"I understand my commitment to you, Twinkle," she says. "If you keep your side of the agreement, I shall keep mine." Then she leaves. It's a bit darker and spookier now that she's taken her hat-light.

Dominique takes charge.

"You must all continue to work as hard as I," she says. "Jess, you must work there." She points in the direction of a big pile of rubble. "Shalini, you must work there." She points to another next to it. "Twinkle, you will work there." She points to a dark corner, away from everyone else. There is hardly any rubble. There is no opportunity to earn ticks. She waits for me to argue.

I don't because I have had another bad thought. What if Ms Thorn doesn't come back in time? How will I know? I have no watch. No clock. No timer! I will have to work really fast and get out of here as soon as we are done. I will not wait for Ms Thorn to come back to me. I will go to her.

"You all have to do what Dominique says," says Arwen. "Dominique is in charge."

"What is it with bossy people?" says Jess. She puts her head on one side as if she is pondering. "Is there such a thing as a *bossy gene*? Were you both born with it or did it just come with practice?"

I suspect the second. I also suspect they will report any lack of compliance to Ms Thorn so I act compliant.

"Fairest Dominique and gentle Arwen, thou dost not need to be bossy. I am yours to command." I'm not. "I am honoured to assist thee in the completion of this Toadspit Task." I'm not. "Thou art both to be

applauded for thy forceful attitudes." They're not.

Dominique tsks again. *Tsk.* Jess and Shalini hide their laughter by turning away.

I change my witchwood spoon into a broom and sweep the bits of granite into a pile. There's barely enough for one block of stone but one tick is better than no ticks so I have a go. I change my spoon back to a spoon and quickly do steps one, two and three.

The dark-grey granite pieces in my zen space light up from the inside with tiny little pink and white glitters, as if there's a sparkler inside each piece. They change colour from dark to light grey as the sparkles reach the outside. The rough edges and broken corners join as if the sparkles are magnets dragging themselves together. The edges sharpen as if they've just been cut by a master stonemason. I set the stone with the right rhyme.

I open my eyes. I have made an ac-chew-all block of granite! I have an alternative to becoming a *Toilet Trainer* should my acting career tragically fail. I can be an architect.

I turn back to Dominique. "Fairest Dominique, I need more chunks."

She's aiming her spoon at a big chunk near the bottom of the blockage. This is NOT a good idea. I warn her.

"Er, Dominique, I don't think you should pull that one out."

"You may not tell I what to do," says Dominique.

"Yes, but, if you pull that one out then the ones above will—"

The chunks of granite slide forward with a horrible crunching noise.

"Fall!"

Jess yells, "Dominique, you idiot!"

The frozen waterfall of rock under the archway is now a tumbling waterfall of rock! A rolling, bouncing waterfall of granite. Dominique shrieks and Arwen screams as shards of stone and powdery dust fill the air and both girls disappear into the cloud.

Jess and Shalini jump back towards me. The ceiling above us creaks. A shower of stones falls between us and Dominique and Arwen. The ceiling cracks and crumbles.

"Look out!" cries Jess.

Shalini shouts, "By the power of the witchwood, by the power of the spoon, I create a bubble with the writing of this—" Her spoon is knocked out of her hand. Jess catches it. I pull them back. Away from the danger. Into my corner.

We're swamped by a whooshing, billowing cloud of dust. Tiny pink shards of granite glitter in our hat-lights. I pull my shirt up over my mouth and nose, like a mask. Jess and Shalini are coughing, bent double.

The dust settles.

The coughing stops.

We are trapped.

Summary:

My life is a pile of dungpats.

My life is a plague of warty boils.

My life is A BUCKET OF STRESS!

We're trapped in the corner, side by side, backed against the wall with nowhere to go because there is rockfall from floor to ceiling. The stones shift and settle and we wait nervously for the rest of the ceiling to fall down on our heads. It doesn't.

"This is bad," says Shalini in a tiny voice.

"It could be worse," says Jess. We jump as a rock shifts.

"In what way could this be worse?" I say. "We're totally trapped. Dominique and Arwen could be dead! And we could run out of air because there is hardly any air in this ridiculously small space that is very crowded and quite squashy and then we'll be dead too!"

"We have light," says Jess. She shines her hat in my face to prove her point. "And we have magic. We just need to solve the problem. Think of a solution." She's looking at me as if I will be the one to come up with the solution.

Shalini is also looking at me.

"Aargh!" I say in response. "Why are you looking at me? I'm an actress, not a problem solver!"

"Twink." Jess is remarkably calm considering our situation. "You are what you are. It's like Mam said when I left home: 'Just be yourself, Jess. No matter who you are. Someone will like the you that is you.'"

"That's so lovely," says Shalini.

"It is," I agree. "But how does it help us? How does it help us save Dominique and Arwen?" I am SO ANNOYED that I am having to ask that question. "How does it get us out of here?"

"What spells do we know that can get us through tons of rock?" says Jess.

"Without bringing down even more tons of rock," adds Shalini.

I wish she hadn't said that because now I'm imagining more rock falling and being trapped in an even smaller space that gets smaller and smaller and smaller until I can't breathe and ... my thumb prickles. I hold it up. There's a knot.

"Uh-oh," says Jess. "That's not good. Make it stop."

"I can't! I'm stressed!"

"But it'll fill the space and crush us!" says Jess. "It'll be Death By Witchwood instead of Death By Granite! You have to shrink it." She grabs my wrist as if she's helping by cutting off the blood supply.

This does not lower my stress level.

"No!" cries Shalini, pulling Jess's hand off. "Let it grow."

"What? No! Why?" I'm finding it difficult to choose my reaction to this suggestion.

"It could help," she says. "It could make a tunnel. It could hold up the ceiling. Like it did in the dining hall to save us from the Slumberous."

"That would need a lot of witchwood," says Jess, as if Shalini's just made a reasonable suggestion, which she hasn't. I was connected to the witchwood tree on that occasion. Now I would have to BE THE TREE.

"Shalini. That is a BAD IDEA. There would have to be more *tree* than *me* to do that. And what if I stay tree once I've passed the fifty per cent tree mark? What if I can't shrink it back because it has totally taken me over!"

"Maybe you don't need to turn totally tree?" says Shalini. "What if we all held hands and channelled the power of your thumb through our spoons to make the tunnel?"

My thumb is now a knotted twig. I can't stop it growing because I can't concentrate on thinking it smaller because they are TALKING! The twig thickens and grows its own twigs.

I breathe in to calm myself. I cough. The air is thick. Staying here means death by absence of air. Staying here means leaving Dominique and Arwen to die, potentially. Staying here means no opportunity to train Ms Thorn. Staying here means no rehearsal and no play. I won't get to play my Bottom. I won't even get to play the *WALL*! I give in.

"Let's do it."

"Excellent," says Shalini, as if she already knows it will work.

"But as soon as we find them we get out," I say. "No investigating, no following strange voices, no opening doors that shouldn't be opened. Agreed?"

"Agreed," says Shalini immediately.

"I suppose so," says Jess.

We link arms. Shalini links with me and Jess links with her. We all hold our spoons out and I hold my thumb out too. It's more than a twig but less than a branch.

"Think of a tunnel," says Jess.

"And think of a rhyme," says Shalini. They're both

looking at me.

"It's your thumb not ours," says Jess.

I think. I think some more but a rhyme won't come. The dust is getting thicker.

"No need to rush," says Jess, which is what people always say when they ac-chew-ally always mean "HURRY UP!"

Aha! I have a beginning. "Witchwood, witchwood, witches three, ask for the power of the tree, to make a tunnel, safe and strong…" I'm stuck.

"Big enough to walk along," says Jess.

Yes! I repeat it. "Big enough to walk along."

My thumb prickles. The prickles pass through me to Shalini.

"Whoa!" she says. Her eyes light up and her spoon trembles.

The prickles reach Jess. She jiggles with excitement. "That feels AWESOME!"

My thumb-twig grows roots. Our spoons grow roots. They snake towards the rubble. They push into the fall, forcing the stones back. Like weeds growing through old concrete but faster. The roots push and push and the noise is like stone scratching on a cheese grater. My teeth tingle. Not in a good

way. There's a space. It expands.

"It's working!" cries Jess. "In we go."

I pause. "I would just like to state that I may be about to enter the East Wing and it is NOT MY FAULT. This is Dominique's fault and if she is not dead when we find her I shall be having very cross words with her because Ms Thorn is bound to consider this BREAKING THE AGREEMENT and a failure to comply with her instructions."

"We'll make sure she knows the truth," says Shalini, pushing me forward.

We enter The Tunnel of Freedom. It's narrow. We go sideways. I'm first. Shalini's in the middle and Jess is last. The witchwood is creaking. The stones are shifting. This is not a comfy place to be. This is a NIGHTMARE place to be.

Shalini's whispering, "Please don't give way. Please don't give way. Please don't give way."

I am thinking, *Stop saying that!*

My shirt catches on a shard of granite and I'm pulled back. It comes loose and the stones move.

Shalini squeaks, "Twink!"

The roots quickly grow over the stones, holding them back.

"If this gives way, we'll be crushed," says Jess. "Totally flattened."

I am now thinking, *Why did you say that?!*

The witchwood twisting from my thumb and our spoons forces its way through the rock. Suddenly there's a crash from behind us.

Jess screams.

Shalini screams.

I scream.

Not necessarily in that order.

The witchwood has let the tunnel collapse behind us! The roots are shrinking towards our backs, over our heads. We are now trapped even more than we were trapped before! We are surrounded by tree-rock! The Tunnel of Freedom could ac-chew-ally be The Tunnel of Death!

"Keep going," says Jess, as if we have any other option!

I say the rhyme again, just to remind the witchwood who's in charge.

We move forward. More tunnel opens up in front and more tunnel collapses behind. The witchwood in front is thinner. Suddenly, the pricking in my thumb changes to pins and needles and it's spreading into my hand and I am hoping it won't spread into my arm and I now I am thinking, *What if I run out of tree?!*

I am choking from the dust and the fear and the panic that we are about to be BURIED ALIVE when suddenly the witchwood opens the tunnel into an empty space and we stumble out over piles of granite chunks littering the floor.

"We're free!" shouts Jess. She pushes us both forward and lets go, cutting the witchwood connection. Shalini's gripping my arm as if she's never going to let go. "Yes, but where's Dominique?" she says. "Where's Arwen?"

"And what's that?" says Jess.

9

Summary:

We're through the archway and Jess's What's that?
*is referring to a large and impressive golden door
straight ahead. But I am not interested in golden
doors. I'm focusing on the fact that I am currently
fifty per cent tree. Fifty-one per cent. Fifty-two per
cent. Fifty-three per cent! This is a guesstimate.
As previously stated – I am an actress not a
mathematician.*

Jess's witchwood is shrinking back into her spoon, as
if the spoon is sucking it back in, but my witchwood
is still entwined with Shalini's so I force her hand off
my arm and break the link with her too. The rocks in
the Tunnel of Freedom shift as their witchwood pulls

away.

Their witchwood has gone within seconds but my thumb-tree continues to grow! They both ignore this.

Shalini searches the rubble for any sign of Dominique and Arwen. There isn't any. Not a hat, a tie, a foot or a hand sticking out from under the rubble. Jess inspects the very large, very shiny, very imposing door.

"This door is amazing!" she says. She's aims her hat-light on it and the light bounces back, giving the walls and floor a warm yellow glow. The door's slightly open. It has silver symbols engraved on the panels. A witchwood spoon, a cauldron, a book, a rune, a key and others. Dark-red words, blood red, have been carved into the stone arch above. *Only The Best And Brightest May Enter The Trials Of Marietta Toadspit.*

I do not like the sound of that. Jess reaches out and wipes a panel at the top with her sleeve. "*Only one will win,*" she says. Shalini leaps across the rubble and pulls her back.

"Do *not* go through that door," she hiss-whispers. "We promised. Plus you can't possibly think it's a good idea to enter a door that has the words *Trials of Marietta Toadspit* written above it. Remember what happened last time we went through a door that we shouldn't have gone through? We unleashed catastrophe and it led to disastrous consequences! We just have to find Dominique and Arwen and get out of— Uh-oh!" She spots me and spins Jess round. "Look at Twink! She's still half tree!"

It's true. I am. I am sitting on the floor surrounded by twigs and roots. They're twisting into a carpet of Celtic knots.

"Twink!" cries Jess. "Stop being a tree!"

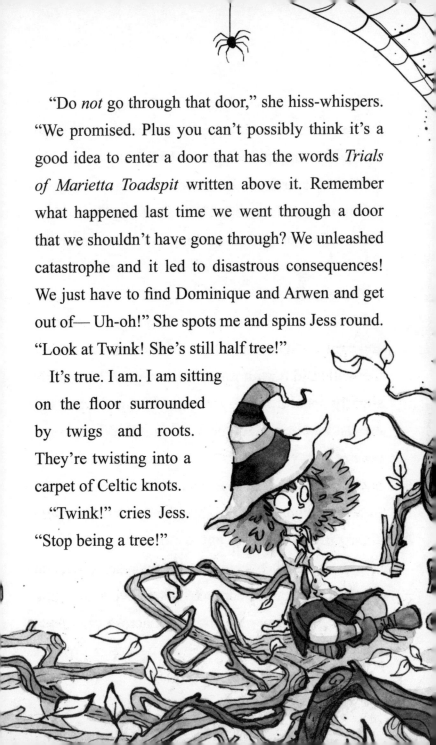

"How can I concentrate on not being a tree when you're distracting me with the possibility you'll go through a secret golden door!" I say.

She moves away from the door. "There," she says. "I will not go through the door. Now you turn back into ninety-nine per cent Twink."

I close my eyes and focus. My zen space is full of roots, twigs, branches and buds. "Witchwood thumb, please hear my plea, I don't want to be a tree. Shrink and shrivel, waste away, be the thumb of yesterday!"

My hand fills with pins and needles. My arm fills with pins and needles. My body fills with pins and needles and I am in AGONY! This AGONY is worse than any previous AGONY ever experienced in the history of AGONY.

"It's working," says Shalini. She sounds impressed.

I grit my teeth and try not to move because moving ALWAYS makes pins and needles worse, and worse would be bad. I hear a creak like a door swinging open. I hear footsteps. Then something like laughter. It's a splutter. It's followed by a guffaw. I frown. I know that guffaw. This is a DISASTER! It's Arwen! There's a tsk. *Tsk.* Arwen AND Dominique! They're ALIVE!

"Ignore them," says Jess.

"Just keep saying the rhyme," says Shalini. "Concentrate."

I comply. I repeat it. I hear Arwen repeating it too. I hear Jess telling her to shut up. I ignore it all. The witchwood in my zen space shrinks. I repeat until the pins and needles have gone and my hand feels light. I open my eyes. I'm normal. I'm exhausted.

Dominique and Arwen are standing in the golden doorway. The door's wide open behind them but I can't see in because they are blocking it. Arwen's sneer is mocking. "Wait till Ms Thorn hears what you've been up to." She pauses. "Twiglet."

Dominique is not sneering. Her look is odd. She's staring at my thumb. She looks annoyed. No, not annoyed. No. She's doing a look from *The Book of Jealousy!* She ac-chew-ally wants to be part witchwood. Of course she does. How can she be the absolute Best and Brightest without a bit of witchwood DNA?

"You are unstable," she says.

She is correct. I am. I am in an emotional turmoil. We are still trapped. Ms Thorn is not here so I have zero chance of bonding and I am furious because…

"This is ALL YOUR FAULT!" I shout at Dominique. "You brought the ceiling down and now you're … NOT EVEN DEAD."

Dominique looks down on me and smirks a smirk from *The Book of Smirks.*

"Twiggy Toadspit," says Arwen. "Twinkletwig."

"Shut up, Arwen," says Jess.

There's a rumble behind us. A shower of stones falls into the tunnel because there's no witchwood left to hold it up. Shalini drags me to my feet and we back away towards the others. More stones fall. The archway cracks, the cracks spread across the ceiling, towards us.

"Uh-oh," says Jess, looking up. "We may have no choice, Twink. I think we'll all have to go through

the door and face the consequences."

"Only the Best and Brightest may enter this room," says Dominique. She nudges Arwen and Arwen stretches her arms across the doorway.

"Get out of the way, Dominique," says Jess.

I get between them. I turn my back to Dominique and Arwen, who are now both standing like Guardians of The Door and hiss-whisper to Jess.

"No, Jess! We have to do exactly what Ms Thorn has told us to do. No exploring. No endangering the school. No causing any disruption at all. No going through any doors! I'll get the blame if anything goes wrong. You know I will. If we go through that door there'll be no need to remember any lines because I will be banned from performing FOR EVER."

I turn back to Dominique.

"No one will go through that door. We will ALL wait here to be rescued."

There's a loud *creaking* directly above us. Oh warty boils! The cracks are spreading. We're sprinkled in dust. Showered in grit. The ceiling is crumbling!

"Look out!" shouts Jess.

She pushes Dominique and Arwen through the golden door and Shalini runs in after them. I hesitate.

"Twink!" Jess is holding the door open. "You have no choice."

Oh dungpats! I give in. As the ceiling crashes down behind me I enter *The Trials of Marietta Toadspit*.

Summary:

I am LIVING IN THE LAND OF ANNOYED! I know entering this door will lead to the possibility of endangering the school and the breaking of The Deal!

Jess slams the door as soon as I'm through. She leans against it and I hold my breath as the rocks crash down on the other side. It holds. Jess grins. I don't. We are completely trapped. I inspect our prison.

The room is round with coloured doors evenly spaced around the white wall. Most have a symbol and some words written in black letters. Three don't: The golden door we've just come through, a black one and a white one. In between the black and white doors is a golden frame of leaves and roses, and inside the frame is a mirror. My face is pale and I have dark circles around my eyes.

The floor is odd. It's made of large triangular flagstones. The points meet in the middle and the bottoms reach the doors.

There's stillness and silence. Then suddenly, there isn't.

There's a rumbly, grating noise, not like ceilings collapsing. More like rusty gears shifting behind the doors of colour. It's a *grumble*. The whole room vibrates. Shalini holds her spoon out ready. So does Jess. Arwen is clinging to Dominique, who is attempting to look unconcerned as if being trapped in an unknown room in the East Wing is not a problem and she is still in charge.

The *grumble* dies away. The mirror's frame glows and the roses light up from within, flickering like red candles. A deep voice booms into the room.

"YOU HAVE ENTERED MARIETTA TOADSPIT'S TRIAL OF THE BEST AND

BRIGHTEST," it booms. This boom is deeper than a Ms Lobelia boom and less friendly. I name it a doom.

"I don't like the word *trial*," says Shalini.

I agree.

"I don't like the word *Marietta*," says Jess. "Uh-oh." She's pointing at the mirror.

I don't like the words *Uh-oh*.

The surface of the glass is fuzzy. Buzzy. It clears and a head appears. It is not human. The head is made of red clay and its eyes are bright green and glowing. I think it's attached to a body because there are shoulders too. It has a round mouth and there's a rolled-up piece of paper slotted into the hole.

"Oh, wow!" says Shalini. "It's a golem!"

Arwen frowns. "You only know that because I wrote about them in *The Toadspit Times*," she says. "I know more than you."

"No one knows more than Shalini," says Jess. "I bet you don't know we found an army of tiny golems in Marietta's Room of Wonderful Things."

Arwen does not know this and Jess knows that she

does not know this.

"I do know that," says Arwen. Jess is about to argue when she's interrupted by the golem.

"ONLY THE BEST AND BRIGHTEST WITCH WILL LEAVE THE TRIAL WITH THE BEST AND BRIGHTEST CHARM," he dooms.

A picture of a silver charm appears in the corner of the mirror. It's like a witchwood knot making the shape B&B.

Dominique's face lights up. She glances at me. It's a glance that says, *That's mine.* I glance back. My glance says, *You are welcome to it.*

The golem continues.

"ALL WITCHES WILL BEGIN WITH THREE CHARMS."

There's a jingle from my bracelet. Three extra charms are dangling. Three silver question marks. The others have them too.

"WITCHES WILL ENTER THREE TRIAL ROOMS. THE CHOICE IS YOURS. ALL THOSE WHO FAIL A TRIAL WILL REMAIN IN THE ROOM UNTIL RELEASED BY MARIETTA TOADSPIT."

"But she's dead," whispers Shalini.

Oh dungpats! I don't have time for this! I have to get out. I plonk myself in front of the golem and act important.

"Mr Golem, sir," I name him Clump, "I have no wish to partake in this event. I wish to be excused. If you could just show me the way out I will depart and leave Dominique to be the Best and Brightest."

Dominique tsks. *Tsk*. "You do not wish to take part because you know you will fail."

"You are incorrect," I say. "I do not wish to take part because I have better things to do." I wait for a response from Clump.

"ANY WITCH WHO WINS THREE TRIALS WILL ENTER THE FINAL TRIAL," he dooms. Which is obviously not the response I was waiting for. The response I was waiting for involved a door opening. An escape route appearing.

"ONLY ONE WITCH WILL WIN THE BEST AND BRIGHTEST CHARM."

I open my mouth to complain but Shalini stops me. "You're wasting your time, Twink. He's not really alive. He can only do and say exactly what he's been instructed to do by the paper in his mouth. The only way to stop him is to take that out."

Oh, dungpats! "But, Shalini, that means I have no choice but to do the trials and I hate having no choice! I am ac-chew-ally allergic to having no choice!"

"CHOOSE YOUR FIRST TRIAL BEFORE THE SAND RUNS OUT."

Clump disappears and a sand timer appears on the glass. The sand is trickling.

I do not believe this! I don't want to choose a trial!

I bang on the glass. "I REFUSE TO CHOOSE!" I shout. Everyone else is inspecting the doors.

Dominique is studying the green door. Arwen's leaning over her shoulder. Jess reads the rhyme on the yellow door to Shalini.

"*If your witch skill is your voice,*
Then enter here, make your choice,
Find a song, a note, or pitch,
To defeat the Qwibbling Quitch."

She looks at me and shakes her head. "That sounds like singing. Plus," she points to a symbol, a musical note, "that's a blatant clue. I am definitely not going in there. You shouldn't go in either. Unless we go in together, with Shalini."

"That's not allowed," says Arwen. She's moved to the purple door.

"He didn't say we couldn't," says Jess. "I think it's a great idea. Maybe we should *all* go in together."

"It's cheating," says Arwen.

"Not if we don't want to win," says Jess. "What about this one, Twink?" She's moved to the red door. It has a cauldron symbol.

I have not moved to any door. I am standing firm in front of the mirror. "As previously mentioned, Jess, I refuse to choose," I say.

She ignores me and reads the words.

"*Add a bit of this, add a bit of that.*

Make a cure for this, make a curse for that.

Boil and simmer, stir and whip,

And maybe even take a sip."

She steps away. "I'm not going in there either," she says.

This is wise. Her potion to cure *Old Man Nose Hairs* resulted in a rather long nose beard when she tested it on herself. Ms Pottage had to intervene.

Clump dooms: "YOU HAVE TEN SECONDS TO CHOOSE. TEN."

"Still refusing." I face the mirror and stand in a power pose. This involves arms folded, legs apart and a look of determination.

"But I wonder what happens if we don't choose," says Shalini nervously.

"NINE."

"Maybe there'll be a punishment," she says.

"EIGHT."

"Or a curse or a hex?"

Jess inspects the blue door.

"Lines connected, lines apart,
Carved and drawn, writing, art.
Make your magic with a mark—"

"SEVEN."

"Choose this door and make a start."

She points at another blatant clue – a carving of a rune above the rhyme. "Runes," she says, just to confirm.

I do not move. I am as solid as the golem.

"SIX."

"I think we should choose, Twink," says Shalini.

She reads the green door. She's rushing.

"Dog and frog, bat and cat,

Bog and log, hat and mat—

"FIVE."

"Which witch words,

Will match with that?"

"FOUR."

There's another *grumble*. I shudder. It's worse than Ms Thorn's sharpened fingers down a block of granite. I imagine. I maintain my power stand. I do not budge.

"THREE."

They all jump as the doors fly open into the rooms. I don't. Shalini falls backwards into Dominique. Dominique grabs her arm and doesn't let go.

Shalini struggles. "Dominique! Let go. What are you doing?" she says, trying to get away.

"TWO."

"I still choose not choosing!" I shout at the mirror. "And you can't make me."

"ONE."

I do not move. I will not give in. I will insist on leaving as soon as the countdown is over.

Shalini's still struggling with Dominique as Clump dooms, "FAILURE TO CHOOSE HAS RESULTED IN – NO CHOICE."

There's another *grumble*, from under our feet. The middle of the floor is opening up. The flagstones tip. I wobble. I stumble into Jess. The tipping tips more! We tumble towards the red door.

"Not potions!" cries Jess, clinging on to me. "Shalini! We need you!" She makes a grab for her but Dominique still has tight hold of Shalini's arm and they're sliding towards the yellow door and the singing trial.

"Dominique!" shouts Shalini. "Let me go!"

"Help!" shouts Arwen. "Dominique!" She disappears through the purple door and I have no idea what's behind that one.

Jess is ac-chew-ally squeezing the air out of me as we roll into the potions room and the door slams shut behind us. The room is freezing. We shiver all

over and our fingers immediately turn red with cold. We sit up and cling to each other as we look around.

I see four iron cauldrons dangling from the ceiling. They're almost touching the floor. There's a table to the side with three dusty bottles standing side by side.

Jess rubs her hands. "I don't like the feel of this cold," she says. Her breath hangs in the air. "It is not a good cold. Uh-oh."

We jump as flames suddenly flicker up the sides of the cauldrons, but that isn't why Jess is saying the *uh-oh* words of disaster. She's staring at the walls and pointing at the walls and her eyes have gone BIG. Almost as big as Shalini's. "I don't like the look of that," she says.

Oh, dungpats!

Neither do I!

11

Summary:

There is POTENTIAL DANGER in the potions room!
There is the possibility of AC-CHEW-AL PERIL!

The walls are made from ice and inside the ice there are thousands of skinny black legs and thousands of big furry bodies and thousands upon thousands of shiny black eyes.

"Toadspit Terrors!" squeaks Jess. She's staring at the spiders as if she expects them to move. They don't.

"It's OK, they're frozen," I say, getting up. Jess follows me. My breath is misting the air as I touch the ice-wall with my fingertips just to make sure. My fingers stick to the ice. I pull them away. "Definitely

frozen. They are dead Terrors."

"But they can't die. Can they?" says Jess. She's just behind me, peering over my shoulder. "Because they weren't alive in the first place. They were drawn and a drawing can't die! Can it?"

"I do not know the answer to that question."

"Well, I think it's a strange sort of way to wallpaper a room," says Jess, backing away towards the cauldrons.

"ATTENTION, WITCHES," dooms Clump. "ADD THE CORRECT INGREDIENT TO EACH CAULDRON TO WIN THE POTIONS CHARM AND ESCAPE THE ROOM."

Jess inspects the three bottles on the table. There's a name and a picture on each label. The labels are faded and dirty.

"We could just fail," she says, squinting at the labels. "It won't matter that much if we fail, will it? It's not like we'll be punished or lose ticks. We'll just have to wait until someone else wins and Marietta lets us... Oh."

That oh is as bad as an uh-oh because Marietta's DEAD and Jess has just remembered that.

"Twink! There is no Marietta! Which means she can't let us out. We could be trapped in here forever because the golem will not let us out because it is not his job and it's not on his bit of paper. We'll starve! We have to win to stay alive!"

She is correct. I act calm in the hope my thumb will believe I am calm and NOT STRESSED.

I take the bottle from her. The glass feels greasy. The label is grimy. There's a picture of a tiny purple flower, but I can't make out the name. There's writing on the back too. The instruction.

"We should inspect each bottle," I say. "Smell each cauldron and read each instruction. Solve each problem and GET OUT."

The second bottle has a picture of a large green leaf on the label. The sort of leaf you rub on a nettle sting. The name is "*Dose of Dock*". We have LOADS of those dock plants around Granny's nettle fields. I am HOPEFUL! I am not IGNORANT. I have ac-chew-al knowledge!

I read the back.

"If prickly lumps be your complaint,

Skin red with sores and itches,

You must make this potion smooth,

To prove that you are witches.

Boil and simmer camomile,

Camphor and aloe,

Stir and whisk from thin to thick,

To make the unguent yellow."

I smile. "Aha! Dock leaf is definitely for itchy lumps."

I pick up the third bottle and read the label.

"Solution of Sage."

The leaf is small and dark green. It looks slightly furry, but that might just be the dirt. I read the back.

"If belly belches and bottom burps,

Are disrupting thy digestion,

Add sage to clove and catnip,

To brew a green concoction."

Jess is giggling. There's a bead of sweat on her

forehead. She wipes it off. I'm warming up too. The fires are getting hotter. "I know someone who needs a cure for bottom burps," she says.

I don't ask who. She tells me.

"My mam! Wouldn't it be funny if sage cured bottom burps because Ms Sage is called sage?" The giggles turn hysterical. I think the threat of Terrors has mushed her brain.

I inspect the first one again. The one that has no name.

"Boiling coriander, caraway, dill,
Lavender and honeysuckle definitely will,
Brew the bluest formulation,
Creating a taste of infatuation."

"Infatuation," says Jess. She says it like this: in-fat-u-ation. There is an increase in giggling. "It's a fat potion!"

I'm not sure she's right. I've heard that word before somewhere. The contents of all four cauldrons are starting to boil already and steam is wafting upwards. The potions are green, purple, orange and brown.

I sniff the orange. Jess does too. She wrinkles her nose up. "This has to be a sort of medicine because, urgh, it smells disgusting, which means it will taste disgusting because medicine always tastes disgusting. It's a medicine rule."

The steam from all four cauldrons is now filling the room. A drip of sweat drips off the end of my nose. "Er, is it me or is it getting really hot in here?" I say.

"It is," says Jess. "Uh-oh. Twink! Look!" She's doing a look from *The Book of Scared*.

I immediately check out the ice walls. They are melting! Oh, warty boils! This is not good. This could lead to a STRESSFUL SITUATION!

"We'd better hurry up!" says Jess. "EEK!" She points at a black and hairy leg sticking out of the ice.

Oh dungpats!

It is TWITCHING!

12

Summary:

The potential possibility of DANGER and PERIL is now REAL DANGER AND REAL PERIL!

Jess is now doing a look from *The Book of Terrified!* I suspect I am too.

"It's all going to melt and they're all going to eat all of us," she says. There is panic in her voice. There is panic in her actions. She grabs the bottle of dock and holds it over the first cauldron, the purple potion. "Does this one go in this one?" she says. "Or this one?" She holds it over the orange. "Which one, Twink? Hurry up. Choose!"

"Why am I the one to choose?"

"Because I didn't grow up with a witch who makes

potions!" she says.

Good point. I try to think. I try to think of Granny's medicine shelves. Pictures flash through my mind. Potions and lotions. Tonics and tinctures. Balms and liniments. Creams and ointments. There were so many! I have it!

"Jess, Granny's nettle-sting ointment is bright yellow and it smells like mothballs. So if any of them smell like mothballs it might be the one that needs the *Dose of Dock*. Which one smells like mothballs?"

"How should I know?" says Jess. "I don't know what mothballs smell like. I don't even know what mothballs are."

"They smell like a smell that moths don't like," I say. I sniff the cauldrons. "They smell like this one." I point to the green cauldron. The liquid's bubbling, the colour reminds me of Granny's spinach soup, dark green and lumpy. "I am one hundred per cent almost certain that we should add this," I hold up the *Dose of Dock*, "to that."

I act certainty in the hope that my certainty is

correct.

"Go on then," says Jess. "What are you waiting for?"

I drip in a drop of dock. Nothing happens. I dribble in more drips. More and more. I empty the bottle. The cauldron hisses and the liquid bubbles and the flames underneath flare up. We step back.

"Maybe I was wrong?"

"I hope not," says Jess. "Maybe we haven't followed all of the instructions."

I check the back of the bottle. "*Stir and whisk from thin to thick.*"

"I can do that," she says. She stirs the liquid with her spoon. It thickens. She stops and says, "Witchwood, witchwood, do the deed. Change to be what I now need."

Her spoon turns into a large metal whisk. She whisks fast and the lumps disappear. The spinach-green turns to grass-green and tiny bubbles form and collect into one big bubble that goes POP and suddenly the green turns sunshine-yellow. The fire goes out and the liquid stops boiling.

"Hurrah! Success!" cries Jess. "One down, two to—" There's a funny noise, like an out-of-tune guitar string being plucked. "Uh-oh. Twink! Look!"

I look.

The ice is melting faster, dripping, pooling on the floor, and hundreds of spider legs are wiggling. Thousands of spider eyes are blinking! My heart

races. My thumb prickles. I quickly say the rhyme and it stops.

"They're *ALL* alive!" says Jess.

"They can't be," I say.

"They ARE!" Jess screams. A Toadspit Terror falls to the floor. Hanging from a thread. It plucks it. A vibration plays along the silk. It sounds like the lowest of low notes on a piano. *Thruuuuuumb*. It dies away. The spider drops to the floor. It creeps towards us and things have just turned NASTY.

"No wonder Greats-Grandma Ursula blocked the East Wing. Marietta was mad to create this trial by torture!" I aim my spoon. "Witchwood, witchwood, do the deed. Change to be what I now need!" It changes into a rolled-up newspaper.

"That's not going to help," says Jess. She changes her spoon to a large net with a very long handle.

She scoops up the Toadspit Terror. It struggles. Its legs stick through the net. "We have to put the other fires out before they all defrost."

She points to where a huge, hand-sized spider is struggling to free itself from the ice. It has ten long legs and one shiny black eye.

"Hurry up and do the next one. I'll take care of the spiders." She turns the net over and over to stop the first spider escaping.

I pick up both bottles. Which one can I do? The purple flower with no name or the Solution of Sage? I fear guessing will be involved. I fear there will be the possibility of failure.

I inspect the purple flower. It looks familiar. Is it one of Granny's? From the garden? From the greenhouse? From the window boxes? I don't know!

"Twink!" The one-eyed spider has escaped. It plucks its thread too. The noise is louder, deeper. *Thruuuuuummmmmbb*. The vibration upsets my heart.

I rub the label, to see if I can clean it and read the name and then suddenly, as I rub the flower, I remember.

"Jess! This might be Oberon's love potion purple pansy flower! From my book. I think. Maybe. Possibly."

Jess yells, "That's fantastic. Stop talking and add it to the right cauldron." She chases the one-eyed spider with the net.

"But even if it is Oberon's flower how do I know which cauldron contains a love potion? How do I know which one is the *right* cauldron? What if I get it wrong?!"

"You're panicking," says Jess, frantically looking from wall to wall, ready for the next terror. "Stop panicking!"

I act calm. Again. I read the instructions.

"*Boiling coriander, caraway, dill,*
Lavender and honeysuckle definitely will,
Brew the bluest formulation,
Creating a taste of infatuation."

I sniff the cauldron on the left, orange. I'm smelling cloves. Granny's cure for toothache.

I sniff the brown. Toffee? Like toffee-apple toffee. I love toffee-apple toffee but would that be in a love potion?

I sniff the purple. I sniff again. I'm getting hints of Granny's lavender patch, sniffles of the honeysuckle around the cottage door. "This one!"

Jess dashes around to the other side of the cauldrons. "There's another terror on the loose!" she screams. "Hurry up!"

I drip Oberon's flower into the purple potion.

"Jess, do I stir? It didn't say stir. Should I stir?" I don't stir. The liquid changes. Bubblier. It turns clearer. Thinner. Bluer. The fire goes out. More success! Jess skids past me, sliding on the icy water. I grab her. I steady her.

"Two down, one to go," I say. A spider scuttles my way. "Eeek!" I jump on to the table. "Jess! There!"

Jess swishes the net under the table. She catches the new spider but loses two others. She swipes again and gains two and loses one. It backs away towards a dripping ice wall. There's another wriggling above it. It plucks a thread with its free legs. The thread leads up to the top corner and disappears through the wall. The room fills with thrumming. *Thruuuuuummmmmmmbbbb.*

"I think he's calling for reinforcements," says Jess. "Uh-oh. He's staring at me!" she cries. "I don't like it when they stare at me. Hurry up!"

I have one bottle and two cauldrons. I ignore the peril and focus on the bottle. Which cauldron should I choose?

"I have sage left and I have no idea which cauldron to add it to!" I say.

"Read it," says Jess.

"*If belly belches and bottom burps,*
Are disrupting thy digestion,
Add sage to clove and catnip,
To brew a green concoction."

AHA!

"It's clove, Jess! Clove!"

I pull the cork out and, after a quick sniff at the orange cauldron, to make sure I did ac-chew-ally smell cloves in there earlier, I tip in the entire contents.

The orange turns dark blue! I was wrong! This is a DISASTER! I have NO SAGE LEFT to add to the other cauldron! I cannot FIX THIS! Suddenly the potion pops with tiny bubbles. As each bubble pops

it releases yellow liquid that swirls into the blue and soon the blue is green and the last two fires flare up then the flames die down and down and all four fires are out.

"We've done it!" I shout. I shout it again in the hope the golem will hear and let us out. "We've done it, Clump!"

"Uh-oh," says Jess. More spiders are spilling

from the melting ice. They're landing on skinny legs, blinking huge eyes in our direction. They're plucking and scuttling and scaring and thrumming more *thrumbs* and I wish they would stop it because it really does sound like they are calling for every spider in the school to join them.

We back towards the door as the thrumming gets louder. Every thread is shaking. It's so loud it's making my heart beat faster.

"Why isn't the door open?" cries Jess.

"We won! LET US OUT!"

Summary:

We are screaming. The Terrors are advancing. We scream some more.

"YOU HAVE COMPLETED YOUR FIRST TRIAL," dooms Clump. I feel a jingle on my wrist; the first charm changes into a potion bottle as the door swings open and we fall out backwards. It slams shut. We are on one side. The Terrors are on the other.

We can't stop screaming but then Jess's screams turn to giggles and she splutters, "It's like Mam says, '*If you're not dead, you've learned something.*' I will never ever forget the smell of moth balls!"

Now my screams turn to laughs. They won't stop.

I believe I am hysterical.

We're back in the Room of Choosing. We are alone then suddenly the purple door flies open making us jump. Arwen stumbles out holding a giant pencil. She leans against the wall and slides down on to the floor. She is not neat and tidy. She is a mess.

We run over. The rhyme on the door is *Draw and sketch to win the test. Survive and you might be the best.*

"D-drawing," stutters Arwen. "So much d-drawing. *Faster and faster and faster and faster and faster before they eat you.*"

"Before what eats you?" says Jess.

"S-s-scarabites," says Arwen.

"Scarabites!" Jess does a Shalini squeak of fear. "Twink, Marietta has set up a Dungeon of Death!"

"This is your fault," says Arwen. She is, of course, meaning me.

HOW? I am about to argue and point out that this is all DOMINIQUE'S fault but the yellow door opens and Shalini and Dominique run out. They're covered in shredded leaves and grey dust. Shalini's hat is lopsided and her plait is twisted round her neck. Dominique is also a mess. Her normally neat black curls are bushy with bits of plant and her tie is missing.

Shalini is ac-chew-ally glaring at Dominique. Her glares are improving. This one is *very* impressive. "You are *not* the boss of me, Dominique Laffitte!" she says. "I do not have to go into every room with you. And I do not want to be part of a Best and Brightest group. Even if I do get a badge."

"Your decision is flawed," says Dominique. "The Best and Brightest must stick together." She's scratching her hand. It's bumpy and red as if she's been stung. There's another lump on her neck. She needs some of the ointment from the potions room.

"I don't care," says Shalini.

Jess looks at me and I look at Jess. We have never heard Shalini sound so cross. Ac-chew-ally, that is not true. She was very cross with us after we broke the Gellica Charm and Doomed the School a few weeks ago. But we have never heard her be so cross with Dominique.

Arwen pulls herself up and runs over to Dominique. "Don't go in the drawing room, Dominique. There are scarabites!"

"And there are Toadspit Terrors in the potions room," Jess tells Shalini.

"Toadspit Terrors!" says Shalini. "Scarabites!" Dominique is forgotten.

"There could be anything behind those other doors," continues Jess. "A vicious veraptor or a swarm of buzzers or a..."

I stop Jess because Shalini's eyes are growing bigger and bigger. "We're all going to DIE!" she says.

Dominique tsks. *Tsk*. "That would not be allowed," she says.

"You're wrong," I say. "If this place isn't deadly dangerous then why did Greats-Grandma Ursula close it? Answer me that."

Dominique does one of her superior looks. "You

are being overly dramatic as usual," she says.

How rude. I am merely stating the obvious. Then, as if to confirm the need for even more drama than the drama she is accusing me of, there's a *grumble* from behind each door and the floor vibrates.

"THE ROOMS ARE BEING RESET. YOU HAVE TEN SECONDS TO CHOOSE THE NEXT TRIAL. TEN."

The timer turns over in the mirror.

"We should share our knowledge," says Shalini. "That way we can all get out of here safely."

"NINE."

"I have no wish to share my knowledge," says Dominique. "I shall succeed and win the charm. It will be proof to all that the Best and Brightest witch at Toadspit Towers is definitely I."

"EIGHT."

"Dominique. You're a twit," says Jess. "This is not about winning. It's about surviving. Your B&B obsession is going to get you into bother."

"SEVEN."

"What if we find a way to turn off the golem?" says Shalini. "He has to be behind one of these doors. She pushes on the black and white doors. They don't budge.

I have a thought. It could be helpful.

"Clump is *ignorant*! He doesn't know who I am. He doesn't know I am a Toadspit. Maybe he'll obey me if he knows that?"

I face the hulk of clay in the glass.

"SIX."

"Heed me, golem. I am Twinkle Toadspit, wearer of the Rainbow Hat of Awesomeness and bearer of The Witchwood Tree Charm." I shake my bracelet at him, showing the silver tree charm.

"FIVE."

"I am the great-great-great-granddaughter of Marietta Toadspit, creator of the Trials of Torture. I have inherited you. I OWN YOU!"

"FOUR."

"I OWN the instruction in your mouth. I order you to STAND DOWN."

"I don't think he cares," says Jess.

"THREE."

The doors fly open.

"I order you to DESIST!" This is a hands-on-hips moment so I put them there.

"Give up, Twink," says Shalini. "It's not working."

"TWO."

"You are foolish," says Dominique. She sends me a sneer as she steps through the red door.

"Typical Twig-twit Toadspit," says Arwen. "It's all about the drama." She follows Dominique, copying the sneer.

"ONE."

Shalini grabs my left elbow. Jess grabs the right.

"Come on," says Jess. Let's do the blue door."

I do not move. I am experiencing annoyance. I do feel as owner, technically, of the school I should be obeyed a bit more by the school's minions. This conforming and complying malarkey seems to all be one way.

"FAILURE TO CHOOSE HAS RESULTED IN –

NO CHOICE."

The flagstones tip again. Oh dungpats! This place is ANNOYING! The centre rises. We slide. Jess holds on to me. I hold on to Shalini but Shalini has one leg on our triangle and one on the next one and she loses her balance and I can't hold her and we all fall and she tumbles towards the blue door as we tumble towards the yellow one.

"No!" I shout. "Not the singing! Anything but the

singing!"

Shalini shouts, "Twink! Just *screeeeeeeech*—"

We are tipped in and the horribly screechy sound she's making is cut off as both doors slam and we are trapped in the singing room and she is trapped in the blue room and we are NOT TOGETHER!

"Shalini!" I shout, as if she will hear me. "What do we sing?"

There is no answer. Shalini is all alone facing whatever must be faced BY HERSELF! I turn around. This room is totally empty apart from me and Jess. No spiders, no scarabites, no vernicious veraptors. Yet. The granite walls, floor and ceiling are cracked, like a frozen puddle that's been stamped on.

"ATTENTION, WITCHES. YOUR VOICE IS THE KEY TO DEFEATING THIS ROOM."

I am experiencing severe annoyance. It's no wonder Greats-Grandma Ursula fell out with Greats-Grandma Marietta. It's no wonder she banished her from the school. She must have turned into a nightmare witch. Evil witch. Demon witch.

We wait for doom to strike. The room continues to be empty. I have a feeling of anticipation as we stand with our backs to the door. This is not a feeling of joyful anticipation. It is a feeling of dreadful anticipation. Which is bigger than scared and slightly less than terrified.

"What's it waiting for?" says Jess. She's scanning the room with her witchwood spoon in her hand. I think she's acting calm. Or maybe she is calm.

"I don't know but I don't like it," I whisper back. The whole room creaks and the cracks widen. "I think something's behind the walls. Trying to push its way through."

"I'm guessing that would be the Qwibbling Quitch," says Jess.

"If your witch skill is your voice,
Then enter here, make your choice.
Find a song, a note, or pitch.
To defeat the Qwibbling Quitch."

"Or what?" I say. "What happens in this room if we fail?"

"Death," says Jess but she's grinning. Why is she grinning?

We both jump at a *crack* from the corner on the left and a lump of granite falls to the floor with a thump and a little cloud of dust. I say my least favourite words.

"Uh-oh."

Summary:

I can stop anticipating something dreadful happening because something is ac-chew-ally happening and the chances of it being dreadful are HIGH.

There's a tiny green shoot growing from the crack in the corner.

"Uh-oh," I say again. There's another thump as another lump of granite falls to the floor and another shoot appears. The shoots grow thicker. More push their way through. The cracks widen. Granite falls. I would step back if I could but, as previously mentioned, our backs are against the door. Which is not a good place to be because the walls on each side are cracking and crumbling and green tendrils are snaking sideways towards us! We jump away. Into the room. We are surrounded.

The plant is growing like ivy, spreading out, weaving into a tangle. The shoots turn into stems. The stems grow leaves and flower buds. It's like a time-lapse film on a nature programme, from seed to sunflower in sixty seconds. Only this plant is no sunflower. The leaves are like nettle leaves, green and spiky around the edges. The flowers are like little silver stars twinkling in a dark-green sky.

"They're so pretty," says Jess.

"And probably deadly," I say. I remember how lumpy Dominique's hand was and how she was scratching. "We need to control it while it's still small. Before it attacks. We

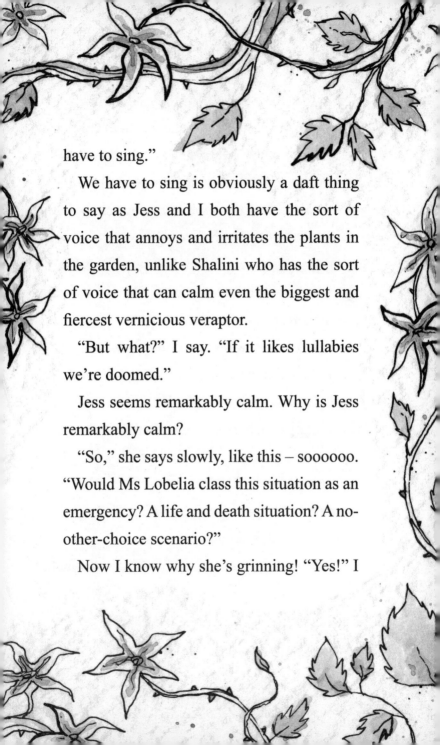

have to sing."

We have to sing is obviously a daft thing to say as Jess and I both have the sort of voice that annoys and irritates the plants in the garden, unlike Shalini who has the sort of voice that can calm even the biggest and fiercest vernicious veraptor.

"But what?" I say. "If it likes lullabies we're doomed."

Jess seems remarkably calm. Why is Jess remarkably calm?

"So," she says slowly, like this – soooooo. "Would Ms Lobelia class this situation as an emergency? A life and death situation? A no-other-choice scenario?"

Now I know why she's grinning! "Yes!" I

say. I grin too. "She most definitely would!"

"I thought so," she says. She is now calm *and* confident. She aims her witchwood spoon at the biggest tangle. "Then this challenge will be easy-peasy. I shall defeat the Quibbling Quitch with the Weedkiller Note Of Death."

She takes a deep breath, breathing in until I think her lungs must be about to burst. She releases the deep vibrations of the weedkiller note.

"*Eeeoooooooowwwwwaaaaaaahhhhhh.*"

The plant shudders. It backs away. I think it's working. The starry flowers jingle against each other as if they're little bells made of real silver. It's a cross sound. An angry sound. A sound of fury. Maybe it isn't working.

"*Eeeeeooooooowwwwwaaaaaahhhhhh.*"

"I think you're annoying it," I say.

"No, I'm definitely killing it," she says. "Watch." She sucks in another enormous breath and aims the note at the tangle growing towards her feet.

"*Eeeeeoooooooooowwwwwaaaaaaaahhhh.*"

The plant squirms and quivers and shudders as if someone's thrown icy water over it. Suddenly, sharp pointy stings spring from the edges of the leaves, like cats' claws. Ready to scratch.

Oh dungpats. The stings are qwibbling with crossness!

"Jess! I think you've just nettled it! I rename this plant *The Stinger*! Ms Lobelia's weedkiller note obviously doesn't work on Marietta's plants." The silver jingling from the flowers is tingling my eardrums. The plant doubles in size.

Jess stops singing and her calm confidence is replaced by PANIC. "But that means we're DOOMED!" she says. "We can't possibly sing properly. That will annoy it even more."

Shoots are growing. Buds are budding. Flowers are blooming and filling the room with jangling jingles.

"Maybe it likes a particular type of song, like Vernon liked his lullabies," I say. "Or…" I have an idea and it might be an idea of genius, maybe not. "It might like old songs. Songs that Marietta would have liked."

"That's an excellent idea," says Jess. "I shall just consult my journal of medieval melodies. Which I do not own!"

"We can make one up," I say. I launch into song and aim my spoon. "With a hey nonny nonny and a fiddle dee dee, I shall sing a song and thee'll obey me. Relent and yield to my tuneful tune … as my words doth cut and my voice doth prune. With a hey nonny noo and a prancing dance, we will win the trial and escape … perchance." I leap about in a silly dance to emphasise the words.

The plant stops shuddering and I think I'm on a winner.

Jess joins in with the singing and the dancing. "Methinks, nonny, nonny, this plant doth be a fool, nonny, wonny, bonny, zonny, dee dah … drool."

Growing has ceased. I feel hopeful so I continue.

"Thou wilt wither and fade away, Jess and Twinkle will be happy and gay."

"Nonny, nonny," adds Jess. "Uh-oh."

The uh-oh of doom is not part of the song.

"Twink," she says. "The Stinger's growing things."

It is. The Stinger is growing nippers, like crabs' nippers.

"Oh dungpats!" I rename it. "It's a *Stingernipper*. Jess, look out! Ouch!" It's crept up behind us and stung my leg. An itchy lump immediately swells up under my tights. It's as big as a grape.

"I don't think it does like the Shakespeare song," she says, dodging a nipper. "I think it was fooling us." She twizzles her spoon. "Witchwood, witchwood, do the deed. Change to be what I now need." Her spoon turns into a wide rake and she pushes the plant back against the walls. The jingling turns angry and clusters of dark-red buds double in size wherever she pushes.

"I don't like the look of that," I shout.

The plant is filling the room. It's growing over our heads! It's tangling together like the tangle of plants in the Garden of Doom.

Jess knocks the stingernipper down with her rake.

It reacts badly. The buds burst open all around us revealing sticky black berries. They're the size of pearls but they're inflating like balloons. The black berry skin stretches and stretches and stretches. Bigger than a grapefruit. Bigger than a melon. Bigger than a pumpkin!

I grab Jess. "I think they're going to pop!" I push my spoon into the air and cry, "By the power of the witchwood, by the power of the spoon. I create a bubble with the writing of this rune!" I scribble the stickman rune in the air.

A bubble of safety forms around us just as the berries burst. SPLAT! The bubble is splattered by sticky, steaming, hissing blackberry juice. Not the tasty blackberry juice that Granny Wart makes. Not the sort of sticky blackberry juice you might find in a pie. This is like blackberry juice with added gloop. Blackberry juice from The Dimension of Disgusting.

"Good timing," says Jess. We hold on to each other so we don't break the bubble spell. She turns her rake back into a spoon and points it towards a stingernipper leaf trying to push its nippers through the magical shield. "Now what?"

I have no idea! We are completely trapped inside the bubble of safety with no way out and no plan for escape and bonding with Ms Thorn is now an IMPOSSIBILITY!

A huge shudder passes through the stingernipper,

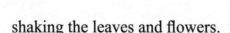

shaking the leaves and flowers.

"What was that?" says Jess.

The stingernipper is shaking. As if something is pushing though the tangle of plant that it is now tangling in on itself and filling every inch of untangled space in the room until there is no more space to fill!

The bubble squeaks under the pressure. Stingers scratch across the surface like extra-pointy fingernails specially sharpened to create extra annoyance. The air feels heavy, as if it's being squashed, like being deep under the sea with the weight of the water pressing down. Not that I have been deep under the sea with the weight of the water pressing down but I imagine it and I don't like it.

A pointy sting stabs right through the bubble and I screech a high-pitched, terror-filled screechy sound because I do not want to be stung to death.

"*Eeeeeek!*"

The sting turns to dust, leaving a tiny hole. The dust falls on Jess's nose. She wipes it off and inspects her fingers.

"What's this?" she says.

"A possible solution!" I say. Another stinger pokes through. I screech again but this time I screech higher. I screech like Shalini screeched as she slid through the blue door.

"*Screeeeeeeech!*"

The stinger turns to dust and I laugh with relief. "We just have to *screeeeeeeeech* like Shalini *screeeeched*!" I screech again as two more stingers poke their stings through. They turn to powder. The bubble is cloudy with dust.

"Then let's do it," says Jess. She lets go of my arm, breaking the bubble, and we are in the middle of the furious stingernipper and I "*Screeeeeeeech!*" because I am TERRIFIED!

Jess joins in.

"*Screeeeeeeeeeeeeeeeeeeech!*"

The stingernippers retreat. We stand back to back and aim the screech. The stings disintegrate and the plant shrivels. The flowers shatter like crystal and the leaves curl in on themselves.

"It's *wooor-kiiiiiiing*," sings Jess, as if she's in an opera. "The leaves are *shriiiiiiii-vel-iiiing*."

I answer her, "This makes me *haaaa-pppeeeeeeee* because we are *wiiiiin-iiiiiiiiiiiiiing!*" The Stingernipper doesn't like the high *iiiiii* notes. So I sing more. My throat feels tight. My neck is stretched. My mouth is open wide, like the time I went to the doctors with a sore throat and I had to say *ah* for far too long.

The plant on my side is retreating, back through the cracks. I stop screeching. It keeps retreating. We've won!

Jess screeches another "*iiiiii*". It's an impressive screech but really it's more like a scream.

She does it again, followed by, "TWINK, LOOK!"

I turn around. She's doing a look from *The Big Book of UH-OHS!*

Summary:

The look from The Big Book of UH-OHS! is not my favourite look and, as previously mentioned, the word LOOK is not my favourite word because in the current tragedy that is my life the word LOOK is never followed by ... at your new cute puppy ... at your giant sticky cherry pie ... at your BAFTA and your OSCAR.

I look. There are eight enormous spider legs wriggling from a crack in the ceiling. They are as long as Ms Thorn's legs! A hairy body is attempting to squeeze through after them. It's squishing. And squashing. And squirming. It suddenly drops down in front of us then bounces back up, like a bungee-jumping scary

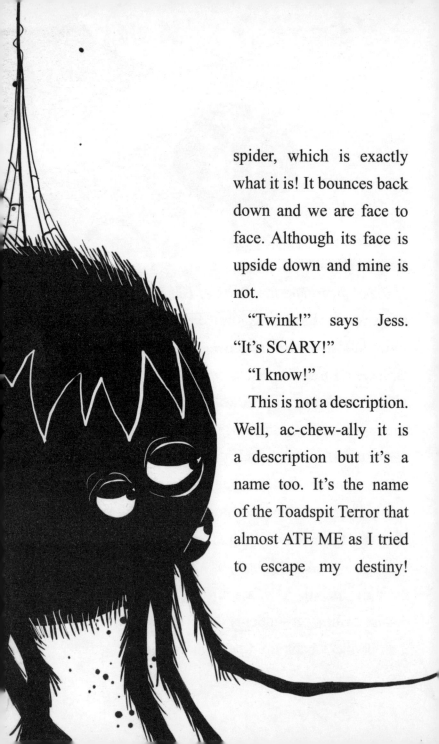

spider, which is exactly
what it is! It bounces back
down and we are face to
face. Although its face is
upside down and mine is
not.

"Twink!" says Jess.
"It's SCARY!"

"I know!"

This is not a description.
Well, ac-chew-ally it is
a description but it's a
name too. It's the name
of the Toadspit Terror that
almost ATE ME as I tried
to escape my destiny!

And now it's going to DO IT AGAIN! Things are much, much worse than they were a moment ago. MUCH WORSE.

Scary is making the thrumming sound from the potions room but BIGGER. It's like this: *thruuuummmmmm*. It reaches into my heart and makes it wobble. It vibrates along the thread he's dangling from and through the hole in the ceiling.

He's watching us with his weird, fractured eyes. We are reflected in bits, like a Picasso painting where all the pieces of the people are there but they're all in the wrong place.

I wait for the attack. The nip. The bite. The crunch. It doesn't come.

He's wiggling his belly, spinning a thread. He catches it with his feet and spins it round and round.

"Uh-oh," says Jess. "I think he's about to cocoon us. What shall we do?!"

"I don't know!" I can't think through the terror. I am frozen. Not cold. Stuck. I am mesmerised by his spinning. He's spinning a thing. A solid thing. He's turning and twirling it, adding more and more silk. Round and round and round it goes.

Jess flicks her spoon and mutters the changing spell. Her spoon changes into a giant fly swatter. She aims it.

"Keep back, Scary," she says. She swipes the swatter at him. He ignores her.

"Jess." I pull on her arm before she can swat him

again. She brushes me off.

"JESS! NO!"

I grab the swatter out of her hands.

"LOOK," I say and at last it's a LOOK that is a *GOOD* LOOK. "Look at the thing he's making."

Scary has stopped spinning. The thing he's spun is hanging from a silken thread. It's a white statue. Of me. He lowers it down. I take it.

Jess stops swatting and inspects the statue. The tiny white figure is doing a look from *The Book of Uh-oh.* I'm not sure this is a good look on me. I prefer a look from *The Book of Everything is OK.*

"Oh," says Jess. "OH," she says again. "But that means…"

"Scary must be my secret admirer."

"Because…"

"I'm a Toadspit? I own the school? I wear the witchwood charm?"

Scary's spinning something else. It's tiny. He takes my wrist. I try not to resist even though the hairs on his legs tickle. He jingles my bracelet. His claws feel spiky but he's really careful not to scratch as he hooks the tiny shape on, next to the witchwood tree. It's another charm. A spider charm.

Jess is doing a look from *The Book of Amazement*. I suspect I am too.

"I do not believe it!" she says. "Twink, you've inherited the Toadspit Terrors from your Greats-Grandma Ursula! You're Queen of the Spiders! A SPIDER GODDESS! Just wait until Dominique finds out." She is laughing hysterically. "She'll explode with jealousy!"

I'm not sure I want her to know, I think.

Scary is attempting to smile. It's odd. I smile back. He doesn't feel Scary any more.

"I think I'll rename him," I say. I touch him on the head, like the queen knighting someone for services to the country, only I use my spoon, not a sword. "I name you … Bruce the spider. Protector of the School."

Bruce nods and suddenly there's a lot of spider clicking and we look up to see other smaller spiders have crawled through the hole. They click their pincers as if they're applauding.

"YOU HAVE COMPLETED YOUR SECOND TASK," dooms Clump.

I look around. All the stingernippers have disappeared. They're all back behind the cracks.

Bruce *thruuuumbs* his thread and the spiders swing up to the corner. They disappear through the hole. With one last weird grin at me Bruce follows. It's a tight squeeze. His legs wiggle through and he's gone.

I feel sad. We were just beginning to bond. Thinking of the word *bond* reminds me of Ms Thorn. Surely if I can make Bruce smile I can make her smile. I have hope!

The door swings open and we race out into the choosing room. It slams behind us. We are alone again.

My bracelet jingles. The second question mark charm has turned into a musical note. Jess has one too. I have a charm but I also have questions.

Question one: Where is Shalini and is she alive?

(Which is tech-nic-ally two questions.)

Question two: What's next?

Question three: Do I really want Dominique to know the Toadspit Terrors think I am a goddess?

I only have one answer. "Jess, I don't want Dominique to know about Bruce. Dominique shall remain ignorant."

"OK," says Jess, just as the blue door bangs open.

Shalini backs out. She's waving her spoon at something in the room. The marks stay in the air as if she was waving a sparkler. Her face is flushed with success. "Take that," she says, and she sounds like a mega-witch of mega-power. Brave and fearless. The door slams shut.

She nods as if she's thinking, *There, that's you sorted*, and then realises we are watching her. Jess and I are doing similar looks. They're from *The Book Of This Is Unexpected Behaviour.*

"Shalini!" says Jess. "That was so cool! You looked like a Warrior Witch."

Shalini grins. There's a jingle from her bracelet.

"I've won the rune charm," she says. She holds up the charm. "I defeated the beastie! On my own!"

We smother her in a hug.

"Of course you did," I say. "Because you are awesome!"

The red door swings open. Dominique runs out. She's flushed, her shirt's hanging out and she's covered in splashes of potion. There is absence of neatness. There is a complete absence of trim and tidy.

Arwen backs out, swishing a broom at a

Toadspit Terror that's trying to follow. She misses. It sees me and stops. I shake my head. It scuttles back into the room and the door slams shut.

I hear Jess whisper to Shalini, "Twink is the Queen of the Spiders now and Scary is called Bruce. Don't tell Dominique. Or Arwen."

Shalini looks puzzled. The word whizzing round her brain is probably *WHAT?*

"Now do you see why we should help each other, Dominique?" says Jess. She looks Dominique up and down and shakes her head in sympathy. This is possibly acting. "We could have told you what to put in each potion and you would not be in the mess that you're in now." She wags her finger at Dominique. "I told you – wanting to prove you're the Best and Brightest is going to get you into bother."

"I do not require your advice, Jessica Moss," says Dominique. She looks Jess up and down and finishes with a sneer; this seems to be her favourite look today. Jess is also the opposite of neat and tidy. Her face is smeared with stingernipper dust. "You

are consistently at the bottom of the green board therefore you cannot assist a witch such as I."

There's a massive *grumble* that sets my teeth on edge and Clump dooms, "THE ROOMS ARE BEING RESET. YOU HAVE TEN SECONDS TO CHOOSE THE NEXT TRIAL. TEN."

"Excellent news, Clump. Can't wait," I say. "Bring it on."

"NINE."

I huddle in the middle of the room with Jess and Shalini. "This time we *will* stay together and get out of here as fast as we can."

We scan the doors.

Shalini points to the red door. "I haven't done potions," she says.

"We have," says Jess.

"EIGHT."

"And we've all done singing," I say.

"And I've done runes," says Shalini. We're all talking really fast.

"What about the orange one?" says Jess. Arwen is

161

standing in front of it so we can't see the rhyme. Jess leaves us and peers over Arwen's shoulder. "It's a zen challenge. We should do that. You're good at zen stuff," she says, looking at me.

"SEVEN."

Arwen puts her hand on the zen door as if she owns it. "You can't go in there. I haven't done this one yet and Dominique might want to do it."

I read the rhyme on the green door, next to the orange door.

"Dog and frog, bat and cat,

Bog and log, hat and mat.

Which witch words,

Will match with that?"

That sounds easy.

"We could do this one, Jess. We're all good at rhymes."

"SIX."

Dominique is at the next door, the purple door. She appears to be pondering. Coming up with a plan to defeat all of us. Possibly.

Jess is still arguing with Arwen. "Well, *we* haven't done zen either, Arwen," she says. "And you're not the boss of the doors."

"FIVE."

"Well, you're not coming in with *me*," says Arwen, standing with her back to the door.

"You are not in charge," says Jess.

"FOUR."

Dominique says. "No. Ms Thorn put I in charge. And I have made my choice. Shalini shall enter the rhyming room with I. You," she points at me, "shall enter the zen room with Jess and Arwen."

She is being The BIGGEST AND BOSSIEST and she's trying to use Shalini to win! Again!

"I will not," I say.

"THREE."

The doors open.

Shalini glares at Dominique. "I won't go in the rhyming room with you, Dominique. I'm going in with Twink and Jess." She steps through the door.

"Dominique," says Arwen. She's still blocking the

zen door and she's doing a look from *The Book of Rejected.* "We should go in here, together."

"TWO."

We are running out of time. I stand in the rhyming doorway with my arms out, side to side, stopping Dominique from entering. She is not pleased.

"Jess!" I shout. "Get in here."

Jess tries dodging round Dominique and it's like a game of netball without the ball but Dominique is really good at blocking and Jess can't get past.

"ONE."

"I will not allow it," says Dominique. "This room is for Shalini and I."

"Get out of the way, Dominique," shouts Jess. "Quick, before we have no choice."

"FAILURE TO CHOOSE HAS RESULTED IN – NO CHOICE."

Jess grabs Dominique and tries to lift her out of the way but Dominique is taller and heavier and she pushes Jess off and Jess stumbles back across our door and lands on Arwen as Dominique falls backwards on to the flagstone that is tipping towards the purple door and she clings to the edge but her fingers slip and she's tipped in.

Then Jess screams, "Twink!" and Arwen screams, "Dominique!" as they slide through the zen door.

SLAM. SLAM.

I am experiencing severe annoyance! We were supposed to stay together! Shalini pulls me backwards into the rhyming room as our door slams shut just missing my thumb. I am shocked!

"Oh dungpats, Shalini. Jess is with Arwen! That does not bode well. What if she fails? What if Arwen stops her winning by being ... Arwen? What if..." I daren't think of any more what ifs. Shalini is trembling.

"We have to get out," she says. "We have to save her!"

"Then we *have* to win the trial as fast as we can," I say. "It's the only solution."

I turn away from the door and inspect the room. The floor is like a chess board. Eight squares by eight squares. There's a word on each tile. That's ... a lot of words! The walls are smooth, which I take as a good sign. No cracks means no creatures bursting through. I hope. "It looks pretty simple," I say. "We just match the words."

"Nothing in the East Wing is that simple," says Shalini.

"ATTENTION, WITCHES. SAY THEM, TOUCH THEM, HAVE A THINK, THEN SAY ONE MORE TO BREAK THE LINK."

A tile near my foot glows red. The word is *yonder*. It's in black. I am feeling rushed. These trials are relentless. There's no time for thinking, no time for pondering. No time for thinking about Ms Thorn and whether Plan A will succeed. No time to think about how much time has passed and whether I have ac-chew-ally run out of time.

"Say them, touch them..." says Shalini.

I bend down and touch the *yonder* tile. I can feel a weird tingle coming through my fingertips. "Can you feel that?" The tingling grows into a vibration.

"I think we should start the task," says Shalini, just as the tile fizzes with energy and turns brown.

"I think we're too late," I say. We jump as the tile goes *CRACK* and suddenly it's like a tray of toffee smashed with a toffee hammer. We whizz round as another tile behind us does the same.

The word is *ponder*. The tiles fizz some more as if the stone is turning into popcorn. They crumble away, leaving two large holes. We hear lots of little plops as the stones fall. *Plop, plop, plop.*

Shalini kneels on the *charm* tile and peers into the *yonder* hole. "Uh-oh," she says, which is ANNOYING. "Is that what I think it is?"

I kneel on *need* and peer in too.

Oh dungpats!

I see THE HORROR THAT LIES BENEATH THE TILES!

I see...

GLOOP!

"It's a lake of GLOOP!" I say. "An ac-chew-al LAKE OF GLOOP!" It's thick and bubbling and extra gloopy and lumpy.

Shalini sits back. She's doing a look from *The Book of Scared*. "So if we fail, we'll fall in and drown in GLOOP!" she says. She gulps. "I don't want to drown in GLOOP!"

I feel another tingle, under my knees. I stumble back. *Need* turns red.

"Quick," says Shalini. "Find a rhyme!"

We scan the tiles for a matching one. I can't see one. Then I do. "There." It's three tiles away. *Feed*

"Say them, touch them," says Shalini. She stands on *need*. I stand on *feed*. Maybe this is going to be easy after all. No! The tiles under our feet turn brown. They fizz.

"Uh-oh," says Shalini. "We've done something wrong."

CRACK! CRACK!

We jump off. The tiles turn to popcorn and crumble. They *PLOP* into the gloop. We've failed and now there are two more giant holes in the floor and this increases our chance of drowning in gloop by ... a lot! I cannot think because I am PANICKING. AGAIN!

"What else did the instruction say?" says Shalini quickly.

"I can't remember. *Say them, touch them, have a think...*"

Another word lights up. *Snooze.* Shalini leaps on it.

"*Say one more to break the link.*"

I see *choose.* I jump across a gloop hole. My toes hurt as I land. These shoes really are too small. "Shoes!" I say, adding a rhyme.

I am hopeful. We have obeyed the instructions. We

have complied.

We wait. Then. DISASTER!

FIZZ! FIZZ! CRACK! CRACK! POP! POP!

We jump off. *Snooze* and *choose* crumble and plop into the gloop. The plops are bigger, louder than the last plops.

"What! Why did that happen?" I am experiencing annoyance again. "We're going to be swimming in gloop before we work out what to do!"

"Drowning in gloop," says Shalini.

A word glows, in the corner. *Spell.* I dash over and put my foot on it. Two tiles away I see *bell.* I put my other foot on that and shout, "Smell!"

We wait. The tiles turn blue. They do not crumble! Success!

"That's it," says Shalini. "Only one of us has to connect the rhymes. With our body. Like Twister!"

Toad lights up. It's near her. She stands on it and scans around.

"There," I point. *Road* is three tiles away. She stretches her right leg towards it. "I can't reach," she says. She stretches. She almost does the splits. Her face is red. There's fizzing. The tip of her toe almost touches the edge of the tile when ... it turns brown. "Noooo," she shouts.

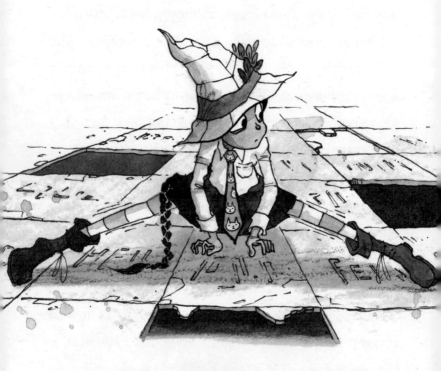

FIZZ! CRACK! POP! Both tiles crumble. *PLOP! PLOP! PLOP! PLOP! PLOP! PLOP!* Shalini's foot disappears into the *toad* hole. She falls forward and her head drops into the *yonder* hole. She jerks it out. "Twink! The gloop is rising!"

I look into the nearest hole. She's right. It's bubbling and steaming and making gloopy plopping noises. Things are worse than they were before!

Shalini jumps to her feet. She wobbles. She balances on *witches* and *spells*. She's surrounded by holes. "Twink, look!" She points.

There's a glow under my feet. *Bubble* is red. I whizz around. There's *rubble*. FOUR tiles away. Not THREE. FOUR. This trial is impossible! I cannot do the splits either. PLUS. There's a gaping gloop hole between the two rhymes.

"Lie down," says Shalini, and I think, *Why didn't we think of that before?*

I lie down. I have one foot on *bubble* and I stretch my arm to *rubble*. My fingers tingle. My head is over the gloop hole. The gloopy smell hits me and I am LIVING IN THE LAND OF DISGUSTING! I groan.

"Twink, think of the extra rhyme," shouts Shalini.

Fubble? Hubble? Gubble? Touble? "Trouble!" I

yell, because that is exactly what I am in. The fizzing under my fingers stops. The tile turns blue. I look back. Bubble is blue too.

"YAY!" shouts Shalini. "Success!"

I get up, avoiding the hole in front of me. There's a red flash to my left. There is no rest. *Lotion* lights up. I spot *potion* in front just as Shalini shouts, "*Motion*, just behind you."

Dungpats! "There are too many. Is it motion or potion?"

"Do all of them," shouts Shalini.

I put one foot on lotion and one foot on potion and one hand on motion then Shalini shouts, "I see commotion!" I look up. She's pointing to my right. She is correct. There is another *otion*!

I stretch my right hand out. I am like a four-legged spider with my bottom in the air. I reach *commotion*. If there is another rhyme I am doomed. I have no more appendages! The tiles are tingling. They're fizzing!

"Add a rhyme, Twink," shouts Shalini. "Potion,

lotion, commotion… Think, Twink."

"I can't think," I shout back. "My current emotional state is one of PANIC. And who can think when their current emotional state is PANIC."

"Twink, you twit." Shalini is grinning. "EMOTION."

The tiles are vibrating. They're turning brown as I shout, "EMOTION!!"

The vibrations stop. The brown turns blue. The tiles DO NOT fizz. The tiles DO NOT crumble into the Gloop of Foulness.

We've got the hang of it. Shalini matches *witch, switch, rich* and *glitch* with *twitch*. I match *ever, never, endeavour* and *forever* with *clever*. We keep going until all the tiles left have been matched but we don't know whether we've won or lost. Do we lose points for the broken tiles? Surely we've won if we're not drowning in gloop?

"YOU HAVE COMPLETED YOUR THIRD TASK."

"Yay!" cries Shalini. The door opens. The last

question mark charm on our bracelets changes to an *R* for rhyme as we tiptoe around the gloop holes, out of the door and into the choosing room. I am exhausted. The room is empty.

There is no Jess.

17

Summary:

We have been alone for minutes. I do not know how many minutes because I do not have a clock. We have listened at each door. We have heard nothing. We have banged on each door. Nothing has happened.

"How long has it been?" says Shalini.

I do not answer because, as previously stated, I do not know.

"What if Jess is dead in the zen room?" she says.

This is not a helpful thing to say.

"What if we never get out of here?"

Neither is this.

"Shalini, you have to stop—"

I am interrupted by the purple door swinging open.

Dominique strides out with a giant pencil-spoon. She changes it back to a charm and hooks it back on her bracelet. She does a look from *The Book of Surprised* when she sees us.

"You survived," she says.

"We did," I say.

She looks around for Arwen and Jess.

"THESE WITCHES HAVE FAILED," dooms Clump.

A picture appears in the mirror.

"It's Jess!" says Shalini.

"And Arwen," says Dominique.

Jess is sitting cross-legged on top of a Bubble of Safety. She's doing a look from *The Book of Very Annoyed*. Arwen is inside the Bubble of Safety. She's looking nervously at the swirling mist that is rising up around the bubble. Shapes are rising and falling. Spooky hands are reaching up. It's a mist of monsters! Poor Jess! What will happen if they reach her? And why isn't she in the Bubble of Safety?

"That is typical Arwen," I say to Dominique.

"Wraps herself in a bubble and leaves Jess to Death By Monster. If Jess dies it will be ALL YOUR FAULT."

The image disappears. Clump's back.

"THE REMAINING WITCHES MUST COMPETE FOR THE BEST AND BRIGHTEST CHARM."

There's a tingle on my wrist. I look. There's now another question mark, next to the rhyme charm.

"YOU MUST ENTER THE BLACK DOOR." It

swings open.

Oh dungpats. "But what about Jess?" I shout. Even though I don't expect it to work I attempt Ms Sage's smile of persuasion on Clump. "You *MUST* open the zen door," I say in an impression of Ms Sage. "You *MUST* release the witches. You *MUST* obey me."

"You are wasting your time," says Dominique. She's already at the black door. "The task must be completed." She steps through.

"Twink," says Shalini. "She's right. We have to do the task. What if Dominique wins and doesn't save Jess? What if she's frozen in the swirling, whirling, scary mist? What if we end up stuck in here forever because Dominique won and we didn't?"

Oh, warty boils. "You're right," I say.

"I know," says Shalini. She drags me away from the mirror and through the black door.

18

Summary:

We have to win the last task or Jess will DIE! And I am bound to get the blame and it will definitely mean detention with some terrible witch punishment that will include NO PERFORMANCES!

Dominique is standing in the middle of the room. She has her back to us. She does not turn around.

The room is bare. Plain white walls, floor and ceiling. No tiles, cracks or beasties embedded in the plaster. Which does not mean there aren't any.

"What was the rhyme on the door?" I whisper to Shalini.

"There wasn't one," she whispers back.

"Then what do we do?" I say.

181

"I don't know," she says. "Wait for an instruction?"

Dominique is ignoring us. She is feeling the wall in front of us.

I move to the wall on the left and copy her. Shalini joins me. I run my fingers over the smooth plaster, trying to get a clue. There is a snort of derision from behind me. It does not come from Shalini.

I turn around expecting a sneer and I get one. Dominique has her witchwood spoon in her hand. She raises it and smiles a Smile of Certainty at me. "You are not the Best and Brightest," she says. "You are the Dumb and Dullest. Only I know how to win this task."

She crosses her eyes and aims her spoon at the wall. She flicks it. Suddenly, there's a *grumble*. It's a big one. A grinding, shrieking, stone on stone, ear-wincing body-shuddering, massive *grumble*.

I look up at the dust falling from the edges of the ceiling, where it meets the walls.

"What just happened?" says Shalini.

"The ceiling moved, Shalini! The ceiling ac-chew-

ally moved! And I don't think it moved UP." I grab Dominique's arm. "What have you done?"

"I have taken the first step towards winning the trial," she says, without uncrossing her eyes. She pulls her arm away and flicks her spoon again. There's another *grumble*. The room shakes. The dust falls and this time we're both certain.

"The ceiling is definitely moving down!" says Shalini.

"Dominique, you *must* stop doing what you're doing," I say. Persuasion does not work on her either. She is not persuaded.

She still has her eyes crossed. It is not a good look on her. On anybody. She flicks another flick and the ceiling drops another drop.

I try bribery. "Dominique, I will give you the biggest chocolate cake in the world if you STOP!"

"Twink," says Shalini. "Look." She has her eyes crossed too. "Look at the walls."

I give in and join in with the cross-eyed look. My vision shifts. I see the atoms. I see the layers. I see something behind the first layer of white. The wall is covered in locks and keys. Big, small, fat, thin. Some with lots of spokes, some with only one or two. One of the keys is moving, sliding across the wall to a lock. It's a big brass lock and a big brass key.

It fits. There's a click. There's a *grumble* and I see a shower of glittering dust atoms fall down. I feel the dust on my face.

I whisper to Shalini, "Maybe Dominique's right. Maybe we have to unlock all of them to get out."

"I'm not sure that's the answer," she whispers back. "Look how many locks there are. There's hundreds. Even if the ceiling only drops one inch per lock we'll be squashed before we've matched them all."

Dominique is sliding another key to another lock. It fits. It clicks.

There's another grating *grumble* from above. Louder, shriekier. Even more dust falls on my head and the dust atoms are flying about like dust motes in the sunshine.

I have an idea. I shall prove Dominique is wrong.

I choose a key. It's small and silver, like a jewellery box key. I find the lock. I slide the key. It fits. There's a click. The dust atoms fly. The ceiling grates a *grumble*. I uncross my eyes. The ceiling is about to touch Dominique's hat!

"Dominique. You are making a mistake. I've just matched a key too. But the golem said there can be only one winner."

There's a flicker of a Frown of Uncertainty on her face. It disappears. "Your thinking is flawed," she says. "The winner is obviously the person who matches the most keys. It is the only sensible conclusion."

Shalini has uncrossed her eyes too. "Maybe there's a special key and lock. Whoever matches *those* is the winner?"

"You are mistaken. The winner is the person who unlocks most locks," says Dominique. "That person will be I," she adds. She flicks. The ceiling drops. The tip of her hat is squished. She doesn't notice.

I cross my eyes again. This is making me dizzy.

The ceiling has touched the top of the highest lock, a large brass and copper lock that would fit perfectly on the heavy Toadspit front door.

Dominique tsks in annoyance. *Tsk.* I wonder if she's just felt the ceiling touch her head. She slides a matching key to the brass and copper lock. There's a click. It unlocks.

"She's wrong," whispers Shalini. "And it can't just be – unlock all the locks and accidentally open the right one. That's too random."

"I agree. We're missing something," I say. I scan the walls. Keys and locks. Locks and keys. There isn't anything else.

There's another *grumble*. I feel the ceiling touch my hat! "Dominique, STOP UNLOCKING THE LOCKS!" I shout. "You're going to crush us!"

"The winner is the person who unlocks the most," she repeats. She is so stubborn! "You just want I to stop because you are losing." Another key slides. She's getting faster now that there are fewer to match on that wall.

I check out the wall on the left. Then ... I see something that does not match.

"Look!" I whisper to Shalini. "There's a tiny golden key on the left wall and it does NOT have a matching lock. It's halfway up. Above the lock to the right of the huge iron padlock. Do you see it? Why doesn't that key have a lock?"

Shalini spots it. "Maybe the lock is on another wall," she whispers.

We scan the other walls. I don't see it. The ceiling continues to drop. My head is bent sideways. I get on my knees and yell, "Dominique! STOP UNLOCKING THE LOCKS!"

"Every other lock has a key," whispers Shalini. She's on her knees too. Our heads are together. "So it has to be here somewhere. But it's not on the walls."

I have an idea of genius! "Then, if it isn't on the walls it has to be—"

"In the door!" says Shalini.

We're right. There's a tiny golden keyhole at the bottom of the white door. It's hard to see because it's so small.

"We've found the key and the lock that will get us out!" says Shalini. She's so excited. She forgets to whisper.

Dominique tsks. *Tsk*. "You are wrong," she insists.

"The winner will be I."

She slots another key over another lock. There's a click and the ceiling drops again. I uncross my eyes and duck even though I am already on my knees. I can't help it. She is determined to squash us!

I sit on my bottom with my legs straight out. "Will you STOP DOING THAT!" The ceiling squishes the top of Dominique's hat again. She's kneeling down now, like us. "You're wrong. We have the answer."

"I am not wrong," says Dominique. "I am never wrong." She flicks another lock.

"I give up," I whisper to Shalini. "We have to get that key into that lock before Dominique crushes us."

"And before the key is covered over by the ceiling," says Shalini as another *grumble* rumbles. Dominique squirms round on to her bottom.

"But only one of us can do it," says Shalini. "And I think it has to be you. Someone has to stop the golem and maybe it needs to be a Toadspit."

Oh dungpats. Why does it always have to be me?

I try to slide the key. It won't move.

"It won't move," I say to Shalini. She tries. She fails.

"It's different to the other keys," she whispers. "So maybe you have to do something different. Not slide it."

She's right, the key does look different to the others. It's shiny as if there's a film over it. Like a piece of see-through sticky tape. Like the gushing hex? Maybe I have to pull the sticky tape off? In my zen space, I imagine peeling away a corner. It lifts. I tug off the rest. The key drops to the floor with a clink. It bounces towards Dominique.

Dominique's eyes fly open. She spots the key. She grabs the key. She keeps the key.

"Dominique, that's Twink's key," says Shalini. She holds her hand out for it.

"The key came to I," says Dominique. She's sitting on her bottom, cross-legged. Her hat is totally squashed and the ceiling is on her head. Her back is straight. It looks like she is holding the ceiling up. Like a Dominique pillar.

"It just bounced," I say.

"It bounced to the Best and Brightest because only the Best and Brightest must win the charm," she says.

"How can you be the Best and Brightest?" I say. "You're willing to squish us to be right!"

The floor judders. There's a *grumble* from underneath us.

Shalini gasps. "Uh-oh! Did the floor move? I think the floor moved! Why did the floor move?"

I have no answer to the word "why". But I agree, it did move. It did not move down, away from the ceiling. It moved UP! If we don't get the key in the lock straight away the lock will be covered up by the rising floor.

Dominique bends her neck and shuffles on her bottom over to the door.

She crosses her eyes. So do I. I see her stabbing the key into the lock. It won't go in. The floor judders. She tries again. The floor judders again and I lie on my tummy.

"STOP IT!" I shout at Dominique. "You are so

determined to win you're going to kill us!" I drag her back by her arm but she keeps stabbing the lock.

"Dominique!" Shalini shouts. "STOP IT!"

She grabs the key out of Dominique's fingers and slides it to me across the floor.

"Give that back to I," shouts Dominique. "The Best and Brightest charm belongs to I!" She tries to climb over Shalini but Shalini rolls over so she's on top and she pins Dominique's arms to the floor.

"Do it, Twink!" she shouts.

I cross my eyes. There's the lock. I push the key in. It doesn't work! The floor judders again. It's a finger away from the bottom of the lock.

"Don't do what Dominique did," says Shalini. She's struggling to keep Dominique pinned. "Do something different."

"What?"

"I don't know. Think, Twink."

I have an idea. I leave the key on the floor. I aim my spoon. I see the key in my zen. I picture it sliding across the floor, I picture it sliding up the door, I picture it turning, fitting in the lock. Click. The door swings open.

I am successful!

The floor underneath me tilts and I tumble out, through the door, into a room of gloom. I drop my spoon. It slides across the floor towards the shadowy shape of a GIANT GOLEM in the corner.

"Hurrah!" I yell. "We're out, Shalini!"

I turn around.

The door slams shut as Shalini screams, "Twinkle!"

Summary:

I have escaped but Shalini and Dominique are LIVING IN THE LAND OF ABOUT TO BE SQUISHED FLAT!

Clump's voice dooms into the gloom, "YOU ARE THE WINNER."

Suddenly I am surrounded by a brightness that is almost blinding. The golem's in the corner next to another white door. He's ENORMOUS. Twice my height. Much taller than Ms Thorn. Much wider than Ms Lobelia. His head is almost touching the ceiling.

The light bounces off seven mirrors on the wall. There's a lever under each. Five levers are pointing up, two are pointing down. The mirrors flash. I see

Jess!

She's alive! She's still sitting on top of Arwen's bubble but the swirling icy mist has almost covered it and I can't see Arwen. Jess has turned her spoon into a duvet and she is completely wrapped up apart from her nose and eyes. Her nose is blue. Her eyes are watering.

The second mirror shows Shalini and Dominique, lying flat on their stomachs. They're arguing. Shalini is pointing at the floor. They're shaking. I think the floor is still rising! Shalini turns her spoon into a thick iron bar to prop up the ceiling. Dominique copies.

Oh dungpats! Jess is about to be frozen and Shalini is about to be squished and I'm the only one who can save them!

"YOU HAVE SUCCESSFULLY EARNED THE BEST AND BRIGHTEST CHARM," dooms Clump.

"I don't care!" I shout.

My bracelet jingles and I have a golden B&B charm in between the witchwood charm and Scary's charm but I ignore that and dash across the room. I have

to lift those levers! I have to release my friends! And Dominique and Arwen.

I reach the first lever but before I can release Shalini I am lifted off my feet by Clump. He's holding me under the armpits. He holds me out in front of him with his arms straight.

"THE WINNER MUST WAIT FOR MARIETTA TOADSPIT."

Oh dungpats! He can't mean that! I struggle but he holds me tighter.

"THE WINNER MUST WAIT FOR MARIETTA TOADSPIT."

"But she's DEAD!"

"THE WINNER MUST WAIT FOR MARIETTA TOADSPIT."

"But she's DECEASED!"

"THE WINNER MUST WAIT FOR MARIETTA TOADSPIT."

"But she is NOT ALIVE!"

Clump is a lump of VERY ANNOYING clay! I reach behind me, over my head, trying to grab the paper out of his mouth. My arms are too short. I twist but his hold on my armpits is too tight.

Oh dungpats! What am I going to do? I need help. Now. I bash his fists but they're solid. My bracelet jingles as I struggle and I have an *AHA!* moment as I spot Bruce's tiny spider charm.

"AHA! Prepare to be defeated, Clump! I am Twinkle Toadspit, Queen of the Toadspit Terrors!"

I unhook Bruce's charm, expecting it to whizz into a big scary Bruce who will destroy the golem and SAVE THE DAY! It doesn't. It turns into a tiny spider that scuttles away from me, across the floor and under the door.

Oh great! That wasn't any help at all! Now everyone is going to die and I am full of STRESS because I can't save my friends and I can't even save me, which is EVEN MORE STRESSFUL!

My thumb twitches a tiny twitch and I have another AHA! moment that possibly leads into another idea of genius.

I think of even more stressful things like I WILL NEVER PERFORM MY BOTTOM and I WILL NEVER BE DAME TWINKLE TOADSPIT or DAME DAISY WART, if I keep my stage name, and then I think the most stressful thing of all. I WILL NEVER SEE GRANNY AGAIN!

My thumb fizzes and it sprouts. I don't stop it. I need more stress! I look at the mirrors.

Jess is now *standing* on Arwen's bubble, still wrapped in the duvet. She's shouting help but I can't hear her. She wobbles. If she falls she'll be as frozen as a Jess-shaped ice lolly!

I feel my stress level rising. My heart beats faster. My skin is hot. I am shaking. There's a much bigger twitching under my thumbnail. A shoot appears. And another. It's working! I look in the second mirror.

Shalini's prop's been squished like a squished balloon that's about to burst. So has Dominique's. They're both lying face down with the ceiling touching their bottoms! One more ceiling drop and there will be squashing!

My thumb is going crazy. It's sprouting shoots and twigs and buds and it's speeding up! I have to control it or my plan is doomed and I'll just be trapped in a room full of tree until I enter the LAND OF DEATH.

I cross my eyes and look in my zen. I see my thumb, the witchwood, me and the golem. I see the paper in his mouth. I twist and turn the witchwood until it reaches the paper. I am hoping this is actually happening and I am not just picturing it in my mind. The witchwood twists the paper out of Clump's mouth. The green lights go out in Clump's eyes.

Clump releases me and I drop to the floor. I open my eyes and turn around. He is nothing but a lump of motionless clay! Success!

I race over to the levers, dragging my witchwood with me because there is NO TIME to shrink it. I lift Shalini's lever. I lift Jess's lever.

There's a horrendously huge *GRUMBLE* that shakes the room, my knees and my tummy. The grating sets my teeth on edge, worse than the time I ate a lemon to practise acting a look of disapproval.

The *GRUMBLE* turns to *GRUMBLING* as the ceiling rises in Shalini's room and the floor drops. The door swings opens and Shalini and Dominique scrabble out, pulling their bent props behind them.

"Twink!" gasps Shalini. "You saved us!"

"You have no proof of that," says Dominique. "You are guessing."

The mist in Jess's room drops as if something is sucking out the air from the room and I hope it's not all of the air that's been sucked out or Jess could die of lack of breathing before the door opens!

Arwen's bubble appears out of the mist. She's huddled in the bottom. Jess slides off, still wrapped in the duvet. She walks over to the door and waits for it to open. She's doing a look from *The Book of Completely Cross and Furious*. Her door opens back into the choosing room.

Now for me. I cross my eyes and say, "Witchwood thumb, please hear my plea, I don't want to be a tree. Shrink and shrivel, waste away, be the thumb of yesterday!"

Pins and needles whoosh through my hand and prickle up my arm. It doesn't hurt as much this time and it's faster. I am definitely the boss of the witchwood DNA.

Everything is going to be all right. At last! My life is a Mountain of Optimism and I am at the top doing a Dance of Happiness because I am one step nearer to getting out of the East Wing and another step nearer to my *very important bonding* and my *very important rehearsal* and my *very important performance*.

"Come on," I say to Shalini. I ignore Dominique. "Let's get out of here." I try the white door behind the motionless golem. It opens easily with just a push. It leads back to the choosing room. Jess is there with

Arwen.

"TWINK! SHALINI! YOU'RE ALIVE!" squeals Jess.

It's hug time. Tears time. A time for relief and laughter and jumping round in a circle. Which is exactly what we do. Dominique and Arwen watch. They do not hug. Although I think Arwen wants to.

Jess sees my bracelet. She grabs it and lifts my wrist up. She inspects my charms. "Oh, wow! Twink! It's official! You *are* the Best and Brightest!"

The B&B charm is all shiny and new and ... mine.

"Only because Shalini is a genius," I say. "She should have one too. And you."

Dominique is beyond cross. She's smouldering. I save her look in my zen space. I call it *The Look Of Absolute Fury.*

My stomach rumbles. It has to be almost lunch time! Almost time to leave for the rehearsal. I have to run. I have to get back to the North Wing. I have to show Ms Thorn that I have the Best and Brightest charm. Surely that will bring a smile to her face!

I run over to the golden door. It swings open. I am facing a wall of granite.

Oh dungpats!

I forgot about the ceiling falling down!

20

Summary:

This school is against me and I am DOOMED!

Suddenly, the stones shift. They slide and tumble into the room. We jump back. Something's pushing them from behind. Something's coming and it sounds big!

Arwen screams. Dominique gets behind her. She's changed her prop into a spoon. She's holding it over Arwen's shoulder.

Shalini and Jess stand side by side with me, their spoons aimed into the stone-filled doorway.

The biggest chunk of granite falls forward and we jump back. I see hairy legs and black eyes and a wonky smile.

"BRUCE!"

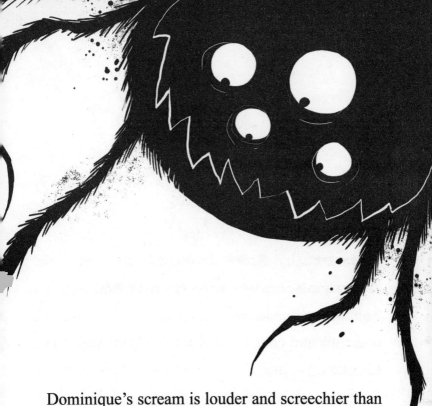

Dominique's scream is louder and screechier than Arwen's.

"IT'S A TOADSPIT TERROR!" she screams.

I turn to her.

"You are mistaken, Dominique," I say. "Bruce is not *A* Toadspit Terror. Bruce is *MY* Toadspit Terror."

I help him out of the rubble and he lowers his head, like a dog wanting a scratch behind the ears. I can't see any ears so I scratch the top of his head-body.

Dominique is now doing a look from *The Book of*

Flabbergasted.

"Twink. Look," says Shalini.

As previously mentioned, "Twink, look," is not my favourite phrase because it is NEVER followed by—

"That's awesome!" says Jess.

I look behind Bruce. Jess and Shalini are at the golden door. They're staring down a tunnel of shiny whiteness. A tunnel made of spider silk. It's glittering with pink and grey. It looks solid. Much safer than a witchwood tunnel.

I smile and the smile turns into a grin as the thought that came with the smile turns into an idea and that idea is ac-chew-ally the best idea of GENIUS I have ever had in my entire life.

I point down the tunnel. "To the dining hall, Bruce!"

I run. I run through the tunnel and Bruce follows with a sort of sideways spider gallop. I hear Jess whooping behind us and Shalini laughing. I have no idea whether Dominique and Arwen are running. I suspect not.

The tunnel ends and I am back just beyond the entrance to the East Wing. I don't stop. I race up the stairs and through the corridors. I have a performance to get to.

I reach the doors. I hesitate. I turn to Bruce and say, "Wait." He does his quirky smile and obeys me. I hurriedly pay my respects to the witchwood and run into the dining hall. No one notices.

The girls are all assembled, ready for food. Dinner has not been served! The grandfather clock strikes one. Time to leave! The maintenance team is at the teachers' table. Ms Sage is at the door to the kitchen, looking dishevelled. Ms Thorn is there too. SHE'S COVERED IN GLOOP! There is an absolute absence of smile.

I run and leap on to the stage. "WITCHES!" I shout. I act important and wait for someone to notice. Ms Sage is first. She claps her hands for silence. She gets it.

I thank her. I begin with a bow and talk fast.

"Fair witches of Toadspit, since the deceasement of Ms Ursula Toadspit," I nod towards my greats-grandma's doll on the shelf, "and the removal of her protections, our school hath been in the direst danger." I add in the *hath* to remind them all I am still a Shakespearean actress. "In danger from Marietta Toadspit's charms, curses and trials. In danger from ac-chew-al granite blocks falling down on our ac-chew-al heads and crushing us, maiming us, squishing us..."

Ms Thorn is ignoring me. She's drying off the gloop with her spoon. I move on.

"Ms Rowanstall and the maintenance team have been maintaining as fast as they can but they are exhausted. Lessons have been cancelled as Essential Toadspit Tasks have been increased."

Jess and Shalini run in. They're panting and glancing behind them with big grins. They give me the thumbs-up.

I pause and look meaningfully at the audience.

"As previously mentioned by Ms Sage, the school was close to CLOSING."

I pause again for extra dramatic effect.

"This did not bode well for the future."

I pause again. Ms Sage approaches. She's doing the curious-eyebrow look.

"However, I have news. I have news of a NEW FUTURE. A future of stability and strength. A future of solidity and sturdiness. A future of creativity and beauty."

I raise my hand and point to the B&B charm.

"I have, with the help of my friends, survived the Trials of Marietta Toadspit in the darkest reaches of the East Wing. I have won the Best and Brightest charm. But that is not important." With a flourish towards the dining-hall doors I say in a voice of joy, "*This* is important. Witches of Toadspit. I give you…" Now for the big pause. "...BRUCE THE SPIDER!"

Right on cue Bruce gallops into the room.

There's immediate CHAOS! Screams! Shouts! Chairs crashing. Tables toppling. Ms Rowanstall falls backwards off her chair. Ms Brambury and Ms Lovage leap up and aim their spoons.

I hold up my hand for silence. I don't get it. Bruce bounces on to the stage next to me and turns to face the witches. He clicks his fangs. Everyone shuts up and freezes with fear. I place my hand on his head-body. I pat him to show everyone that I am the Queen of the Spiders. I briefly wonder whether a prop is needed. A crown? A tiara. People are restless. I perform.

"Witches of Toadspit! Behold Bruce! The spinner of silk. The spinner of strength. The spinner of

awesomeness! The SAVIOUR of Toadspit Towers!"

There are so many LOOKS. Looks of fear. Looks of fright. Looks of terror. Looks from *The Book of I am Scared of the HUGE SCARY SPIDER!*

They're just beginning to settle down when we hear screaming from the corridor and Dominique and Arwen dash into the hall. Their screaming is LOUD because they're being chased by an ac-chew-al army of Toadspit Terrors!

We have chaos again. Screaming can get *very* annoying and now there's also mayhem and madness! The witchwood cats are meowing their flutey meows. They're leaving the roots, joining the girls and teachers as if they're trying to calm them down. Oddbod jumps on to the stage and leaps into my arms. I catch him. He leans forward and sniffs Bruce, tickling him with his whiskers. He's purring.

Dominique and Arwen dash to Ms Thorn. They're jibbering and jabbering and pointing at me. Ms Thorn does the curious-eyebrow look at them and then she aims it at me and Bruce and Oddbod. I name it the extremely-curious-eyebrow look. There is still an absence of smile but no one would smile if they've just been covered in gloop.

Jess and Shalini join them and now *they're*

jibbering and jabbering and pointing at me. Ms Thorn holds her hand up and they all stop talking. They take a step back. She points her spoon at the rest of the gloop covering her outfit, it changes to dust and she brushes it off. She's still looking at me. There is still an absence of smile.

I suspect Ms Thorn is allergic to chaos. I must stop the chaos. I face Bruce. I stare into his eyes. All of them. I cross my arms, tap my foot and raise my eyebrow. He understands. He clicks his nippers once. The army of spiders gather behind us on the stage. He clicks once more. They sit down, like well-trained dogs. Legs crossed neatly. The screaming drops to whimpering.

I keep one hand on Bruce's head-body and I cross my eyes. I picture a picture in my zen space. I uncross them. I see the picture in Bruce's eyes. He blinks and it's gone. He's ready. So am I.

I open my arms to the audience. "Witches. Behold the power of the Toadspit Terrors!" I step back. "BRUCE! SAVE THE SCHOOL!"

Bruce retreats to the back of the stage, the smaller spiders move sideways. He clicks instructions. The spiders fan out across the walls, avoiding the windows and the doors, the witchwood and the dolls.

Bruce spins. One, two, three … eight threads. The terrors catch them and pass them, pulling, twisting, sticking, webbing thinner silken threads between the thick threads. Bruce plucks the web and the air fills with thrumming. ***Thruuuummmmmmbbbbb.***

I cross my eyes and look beyond. The silk is sinking into the granite. Bonding with the stone. Weaving through the atoms.

I hear gasping. I hear whispering. I hear laughing. I hear clapping and I open my eyes.

It's working! The spiders are spreading out across the stone. More spiders are joining in. They're crawling out of every crack, scuttling from the witchwood roots and the *thruuuuummmbing* grows louder and louder and louder and I am filled with joy.

There's no more crumbling granite. No more falling-down building. Just strong, smooth, silky walls of sparkly white, grey and pink. The sunshine shining through the stained-glass windows and doors lights up the walls with pictures and patterns that shift and change as if a breeze is blowing.

Ms Lobelia dashes through the garden

doors. "What's happening to the school?" she booms. "The towers are turning white and..." Her voice trails away as she sees the spinning spiders and the colours drifting across the walls. The spiders are transforming the hall from a crumbling, derelict building into a hall of magnificence.

Ms Lobelia is doing a look from *The Book of THIS IS AWESOME!* She throws back her head and booms, "THIS IS AWESOME!"

The room erupts with laughter.

Ms Sage is clapping and clapping like a sea lion who's just seen a bucket of cod. And Ms Thorn...

...is giving me the oddest look.

It isn't a smile.

It isn't a grin.

I think it's...

Gratitude... Pleasure... Happiness!

And ... it's gone.

Ms Sage distracts me. She climbs on to the stage. She grabs me. She hugs me. She turns to the girls. There's jumping up and down with excitement as Bruce and the spiders spin across the ceiling.

Jess and Shalini join us. We're all gawping upwards.

"Oh, how wonderful!" says Ms Sage. "How perfectly stupendous! Twinkle Toadspit has Saved the School just like I knew she would. We shall all

eat CAKE!"

I am just about to say OR PIE, when I look down and see Ms Thorn approaching the stage, followed by Dominique and Arwen. Shalini and Jess dash in front of them. They both look anxious.

Ms Thorn stands in front of the stage and our heads are level. She looks me straight in the eyes.

"Dominique and Arwen have provided a full report on the situation in the East Wing," she says. Dominique is smirking. I do not believe this! Is she still trying to get me into trouble?

Jess and Shalini step between us.

"But Ms Thorn," says Shalini. "We reported too."

"They're lying," says Jess. "Whatever they've said, they're lying."

Ms Thorn ignores them. She looks over their heads at Ms Sage. "Twinkle will not have cake, Ms Sage," she says.

What! I am too indignant to act anything but indignant. "Ms Thorn, I must protest. I—"

Ms Thorn stops me. She raises her hand and her

eyebrow. "Twinkle will not have cake because she does not have time for cake."

"But—"

"We must leave for the theatre," she says. She hesitates and then there's a tiny, tiny hint of a smile as she adds, "Twinkle has kept her side of the deal she made. She has not endangered the school. In fact, she has saved the school. I shall accompany her to her rehearsal and performance."

"Yes, she has! Indeed she has," says Ms Sage. She does more of her sea lion clapping of happiness. "I don't know how, but I'm sure Jess and Shalini will tell me."

Jess and Shalini jump up on the stage and there is more hugging.

"Break a leg," says Jess.

"That means good luck," says Shalini. "Don't do it really." She lets go and turns to Ms Thorn. "Ms Thorn. What about the toilets? Should we finish the toilets?" She really is obsessed. "If we don't finish them the hex will spread and—"

Ms Sage interrupts.

"Oh, I'm sure Dominique and Arwen would be more than happy to take over that particular task while you tell me exactly what happened to cause this amazing transformation," she says.

Dominique and Arwen both do a look from *The Book of DUNGPATS AND WARTY BOILS!*

"But, Ms Sage," says Dominique.

"Off you go," she says. "You *must* begin now if you are to finish before bedtime."

They cannot resist Ms Sage's power of persuasion. They leave. They do not strut. The do not swagger. They do the *walk of failure.*

Ms Thorn is looking at me. She's tapping her cane.

"Come along, Twinkle," she says. "You have a rehearsal to attend and a performance to perform. We must not be late." She pauses and then adds, "Strangely, now that the school has been saved, I find I am actually looking forward to being amused by your Bottom."

This time I definitely do see a smile.

I smile back.

22

Summary:

My rehearsal was the best rehearsal EVER.

Ms Thorn was amused. There was a hint of a look from The Book of Happiness *and she even APPLAUDED!*

I was not demoted to the WALL.

My thumb did not turn into a tree.

That night I performed my Bottom on an ac-chew-al stage in an ac-chew-al theatre and it was ac-chew-ally MAGNIFICENT!

Acknowledgements

I'm going to put family first in this batch of thank yous. Geoff, Katherine and Andy, Chris and Hannah. Thank you for your support, for allowing me to ignore you, for feeding me, for being patient, for believing in me, for being proud of my achievements and for loving me. I love you more than chocolate.

Big hugs go to agent Amber Caraveo for matching me up with the Nosy Crow team. Huge thanks to you all, especially Kirsten Stansfield, Fiona Scoble, Nicola Theobald, Rebecca Mason, Catherine Stokes, Hester Seddon and Kate Wilson for believing in Twink and working so hard to publish three books in just over a year! An awesome achievement! Hugs to Jamie Littler who once again has made me laugh with his illustrations of Twink and the gang. My favourite this book? Obviously I love the hug image but Shalini doing the splits really made me giggle.

The SCBWI BI group continues to be amazing with so many friends and colleagues sharing and recommending Witch School. Thank you!

My last big shout out goes to Angela Morton (Knitting Yarns) and the Saltburn Knitters for helping with the Awesome Toadspit Hats and featuring Get Me Out of Witch School! as part of their yarn bombing. That was a career highlight!

LOOK OUT FOR

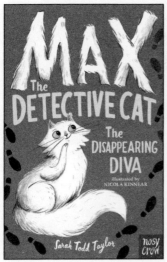
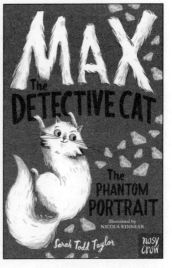

He's the clever cat who puts
the miaow into mystery!

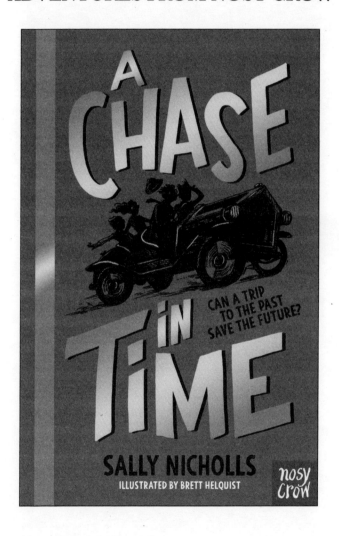

MORE FUNNY FICTION
FROM NOSY CROW